Dickens and the Whore

Jennifer M. Emerson

Dickens and the Whore

Copyright © 2013 Jennifer M. Emerson, Petticoat Press

www.jennifermemerson.weebly.com

All rights reserved. No portion of this publication may be reproduced or distributed – mechanically, electronically or by any other means, including photocopying and recording – without the written permission of the author/publisher.

ISBN-13: 978-1499180022
ISBN-10: 1499180020

Photography and Design: Jennifer M. Emerson

Printed in the United States of America

Author's Note.

Though inspired by the story of Urania Cottage, an actual London Home for fallen women conceived by Charles Dickens and opened in 1847, this novel is a work of fiction. And though many of the characters were real people, I have taken liberties with them, which, I hope, will be pardoned by both the Academe, and the Here After. My intent was to give a dramatized account of the early days of this unique social experiment through the eyes of a girl who lived it, and delve into the inner workings of the man who felt it possible to offer such women an innovative second chance.

If, after turning the last page, my readers feel they know Charles Dickens and the Girls of Urania Cottage in a fuller and more compelling fashion, I will consider my duty done.

Jennifer M. Emerson – December, 2013

"...*the tendency is all downwards.* The case is, in this respect, *unique.* Even in thievery, there may be an advance...But in the present case, *rising is a thing unknown.*
It cannot be. It is all descent."

~Ralph Wardlaw.
Lectures on Female Prostitution, 1842.

"The design is simply...to appeal to them by means of affectionate kindness and trustfulness...
Dealing gently...These unfortunate creatures are to be tempted to virtue."

~Charles Dickens.
Letter to Angela Burdett Coutts, 1847.

"Still govern thou my song, Urania, and fit audience find, though few."

~John Milton.
Paradise Lost, 1667.

PROLOGUE

WESTMINSTER ABBEY, LONDON
13 JUNE, 1870.

Other than the clacking of shoes on cool, aged stone, the only sound was weeping. Some wept openly, others attempted to stifle their outbursts in their handkerchiefs, aprons or even their hands. But I cared not about them, or what they felt.

It seemed a sea of people, of all stations. Gentlemen in suits of black, their Ladies in their bustle gowns (hoops were on the out, giving rise to a new, more sleek fashion) clutching their escort's arm as if they might faint. Today I have put the rules of fashion aside; I have not come in black. He would not have wanted that. The colour of my gown is particular. My last—nay, my only gift to *him.*

Working people were dressed in their best, some with children. Many held bouquets—some were from immaculate gardens or florist carts and tied in silk ribbons. Others had clearly been pinched from wherever they could be found.

In front of me, a man dressed in a threadbare brown suit, greatly thinned at the elbows, was flanked on either side by a child, whose hands he was holding—a boy of about seven and a girl of about five. They were likewise thinly clad, wearing scuffed, worn shoes that would soon be too small for them. The boy's toes were nearly visible through the now greyed leather they sat directly under. The father spoke gently to his two children as they approached the grave.

"Remember this day, my dears. A great man; a friend, has left us."

As the queue processed, ancient statues kept watch. Did they know, I wondered, or did they approve of this throng of intruders in their realm? Perhaps they did. Like them, my cheeks were smooth; unkissed by grief. The tears had all been spent long ago.

A cascade of flowers obscured the maw of the still open grave. The coffin was in there, though, somewhere. The father, a few paces in front of me, brought his children to the edge of the flowering pile. In their hands they each held a small bouquet of wildflowers, which were bound by bits of old, yellowed cloth.

"Go on, my darlings," said the children's father with an encouraging pat on their shoulders. The children each tossed their tiny, ragged bouquets into the pit.

"Will he like them, Pa?" asked the boy.

"Of course he will, David," replied his father, gently.

The little girl began to sniffle and turned her face into her father's leg.

"Oh, now, my pet," cooed her father, "Don't you cry."

The girl wiped her nose on her hand and looked up at him, "Is he in Heaven?"

"No doubt about it, my little Em'ly," replied his father with a wink, "if ever a man was worthy of it.

Now, let's go home and tell your mother all about what we've done today."

I smiled. *She's not Little Em'ly. I am.*

They walked away and turned left at the high altar to exit the Abbey down its long main corridor, the little girl still sniffling a bit. Now I stood before the open grave, my own small bouquet in my hand. Then I looked around me.

Did your hear that, Dandy? Them children was named for characters you penned—that I helped you to pen. Well, let us see who your new neighbors are. Handel at your head, Chaucer and Byron nearby; a statue of Shakespeare looking down at you. Fine company to spend eternity with, I dare say, Dandy, ain't it?

"Please move on, Madam," said a gentle voice behind me. It was a man clad in a sort of Minister's robes. The long dark cotton garment had been freshly ironed.

"I already have," I responded as I turned in his direction, "I only wanted to say goodbye to him."

He gave me a puzzled look. "Pardon me, but am I to assume that you knew *him*, Madam?" asked the clerical man as he gestured toward the grave.

A shiver came upon me as I looked down to where my flowers now rested, and I closed my eyes.

"A lifetime ago," I whispered.

CHAPTER I

A DARK NIGHT IN LONDON. SEPTEMBER, 1847— IN WHICH A YOUNG WOMAN'S FATE IS UNCERTAIN.

When I felt the man's hands clutching my shoulders, pulling me, I knew which way I had gone. Hell. But then I became aware of a light that seemed to dangle over me. The added penitent sensation of rocking back and forth would, I had thought, have suggested Heaven. But it could not possibly have been so cold and wet there.

"She moved," a voice said in surprise.

"Turn her over, quick Matt, so she pukes over the gunwale," ordered another gruffer voice.

A torrent of thick, foul water surged from my gut and out of my mouth, tasting of shit and coal. Thick strong fingers entwined with my hair, lifting my head up. I cried out at the sharp aches in my back and crotch.

"Did you jump, child?"

I forced open my eyes and in the lamplight beheld the face of a young man. He was handsome, but reeked of fish and oakum, as did his woolen coat. His green eyes and matted black hair looked as if he had not had a proper wash in months. I tried to speak, but instead returned more of Father Thames back into him. When I had finished, the young man guided me down on to the bottom of the small boat. But instead of feeling rough wood, I had come to rest on something wet, soft and stinking. A spasm of pain thundered through me, and I clutched the nearest thing to hand. The oyster-like feel of it made me look at what I had grasped. It was a hand. I lay atop a corpse.

The younger man wiped my long, soiled hair back from my face. "Sorry it's a bit crowded in here. If we hadn't come along when we did, that would've been you. Poor girl, you've had a rum go of it, haven't you? Lucky I saw you." Then he turned his attention to the older man seated at the stern, cloaked in pipe smoke. "Pretty, ain't she, Tom? I reckon she fell from Waterloo Bridge; we're nearly under it now."

"Aye," said Tom. The lamp cast frightening shadows and framed him in an amber countenance. He had a coarse, grey beard and eyes like two black buttons. His great coat, shoes and trousers were like the rest of him, tattered and mud stained. His words slurred through the pipe between his yellow teeth, "Someone's given her a right going over. Too bad for her and us we come along so soon; we could've had two dead'un's tonight. No matter, the Traps will part with a few coins for this little cockpinch. Where shall she go, I wonder? Pentonville, perhaps? Aye."

Matt sat back down on the nearby thwart, causing the boat to lurch as hard as my stomach. "I'd as soon cast her back in than send her to prison, Tom. Why not take her to The Magdalen? We could get there by way of Blackfriars Bridge, and it ain't that far. I hear they treat them pretty well there."

"Bugger it all if your head ain't turned by every petticoat you meet, Matt!" howled the older, gruffer voice. "You know this girl?"

"Seeing as she's covered in muck, I can't rightly tell. Besides, it ain't as if you've never been up a bit of skirt in your time, Tom."

The old man spat at me.

"What's she to you, lad?"

"Nothing, Tom."

"Well then," said Tom, pointing down to me with his pipe, "what's one less whore?"

"She ain't the only one what's got sins. You and me rob the dead for money."

Tom chortled. "Sin? We've got a right to eat, don't we?"

Matt leaned down and wiped my mouth with his handkerchief.

"So don't she, Tom."

Tom dug in his ear with the little finger of his right hand, "Alright, there's another prison I know of what's got an infirmary. We'll take her there. Now make yourself useful and clap onto them oars. Make for the Westminster Steps. Mark me, boy, this is the first and only time I let you go fishing with me."

"I understand," Matt said. He leaned down close to me, "You'll be safe there. I'll tell *him* where you are." Then he exchanged places with Tom.

My tongue, unable to make a sound, might as well have been in the mouth of the icy form crumpled beneath me. Her clear, empty eyes bulged out from her swollen face, as if she was astonished to behold me there. I touched her sponge-like cheek, and laid my head on her breast in a silent plea to join her.

Had I the strength, I would have begged those men to give me back to the Thames. But soon I could hear the motion of the oars as Matt rowed toward my certain doom. Tom's coarse beard grazed my ear as he exhaled smoke in my face. His putrid breath and grating voice taunted me in a harsh whisper.

"It's Tothill Fields for you, Cunny."

CHAPTER II

THE EVENTS OF SEVERAL DAYS BEFORE, IN WHICH THE SECRET SENTIMENTS OF MR. CHARLES DICKENS, OF 1 DEVONSHIRE TERRACE, ARE BROUGHT TO LIGHT.

She appeared through the mist, clad in white gossamer. Her dark hair hung loosely, framing her porcelain face. Her form was as unchanged as her smile. It was the smile that had inspired me to pick up my pen, and that had told me the secrets of her heart.

"My dearest Charles," she whispered.

The smell of her fragrance swam over me. I held my arms out eagerly to embrace her, but she was just beyond my reach.

And then she vanished.

I shot straight up in bed quick as a lightning bolt. My arms groped the empty black air in the vain hope that I could pull her from my dream back into life. But she was gone. I buried my head in my hands. My eyes were tightly closed. Overcome with emotion, I managed to choke out one hushed whisper into the darkened chamber.

"Mary."

I swung my legs over the side of the bed and sat for a moment, still half dazed. It had been over ten long years now since Mary had died. My Mary. My Angel. It may sound strange for a man to apply such a term to a sister-in-law, but Mary was an angel; as perfect a being as ever walked this earth. God had seen fit to part us. Whether it was a punishment to me, I could only speculate.

The feel of her lying limp in my arms was as fresh as if it had happened yesterday. I had continued to hold Mary long after she had grown cold, and would have been content to do so for eternity. But I never told my wife that. Our old house in Doughty Street had been plunged into an insurmountable abyss of grief at the loss of our dear Mary. My wife Catherine had borne her younger sister's death surprisingly well. The shock had resulted in a miscarriage, but she had recovered and shown her resilience. And I, of course, adored my wife. But truthfully it wasn't the same since Mary had gone.

My left hand trembled as I raised it to my lips and kissed the small ring on my little finger. On that long ago melancholy day, I had removed it from Mary's lifeless hand and placed it on mine, never to be removed. Even unto death.

It took four attempts to finally light the candle on the night stand and lift my pocket watch. Seven minutes to twelve. Since it was now evident that the fickle arms of Morpheus would deny me any further respite, I rose from the bed. It was always the same when sleep would not come, which was often. Work. Walk. Observe. Write. That was the only remedy. Others called it restlessness. To me, it is compulsion.

The Muse is a fickle Siren. But she had bestowed great favor upon me. Everyone read my stories. Everyone. I was known throughout the world.

Even the Americans, damn the bloody pirates, loved me: The Inimitable. However, Muse set her price high. Enslavement to a life of work. Of recompense.

I lit the small oil lamp and snuffed out the candle. Then I dressed myself, took lamp in hand, and crept to the door. My hand had wrapped around the doorknob when I heard my wife's drowsy voice.

"Charles?"

I sighed and crept back to her side of the bed.

"I'm just out for a walk," I answered softly as I kissed her cheek. "Go back to sleep."

A muffled assent was my wife's only reply, quickly followed by soft snoring. She needed her rest. Sydney had been born but five months ago. Now she was expecting again. This next child would make eight. Eight. Catherine seemed to become pregnant if I walked into the same room with her. Had I not yet done sufficiently toward my Country's surplus population?

In the darkness of the splendid house I felt stifled. I craved light; I always had. There was a marbled-topped table near the front door where I set down the lamp and donned a heavy brown coat and a grey felted hat with a broad rim. An actor must have the proper costume for the part, especially when he wishes to walk unnoticed.

The lamp cast enough light for me to view my visage in the opulent mirror that hung above the table. I passed a hand over my mouth. The new fashion for Gentlemen was to grow whiskers. But, ever true to the lost era of my youth, I had resisted that. It would make me look older than my thirty-five years. And that, in short, would never do.

The timid patter of two tiny slippers on the black and white tiled floor interrupted the contemplation of beards.

"Papa?" a small voice whispered behind me.

I turned and knelt down, taking my daughter's hands in mine.

"Papa is going out for a walk, Katey. No need to worry your pretty head, which, along with the rest of you, should be in bed."

A wide pair of eyes and a dash of red hair gazed at me from under a tussled cap. She resembled me a great deal.

"Why don't you walk when it's light, Papa?"

I smiled. Katey would ask about the light. Numerous and ever growing as they were, I loved my children, and had bestowed them all with colorful nicknames. Charlie was 'Flaster Floby', Maimie was 'Mild Glo'ster', Walter was 'Young Skull', Frank was 'Chicken Stalker', and Alfred was 'Skittles'. Our new Sydney would be 'Ocean Spectre'. But Katey had a clever spark, and was fiery, like me. This had earned her the title of 'Lucifer Box'.

"Because night opens secrets that hide from the sun, my dear," said I.

"Will you be home to breakfast with us, Papa? I have another drawing for you."

I tapped her nose with the tip of my finger. "I shall be there, and I look forward to perusing your drawing. Now, Lucifer Box, back to bed, or we will be eating you for breakfast. And then we'll pick your bones."

I licked my lips and inched toward my daughter, my fingers clawing the air in a tickling motion. Her soft giggles grew louder, and I gathered her into my arms to quiet her.

"Careful," I whispered, "or Aunt Georgy might hear. She'd be cross if she found you awake so late."

"Yes, Papa," said Katey. I kissed her cheek and she scurried quicker than a mouse along the tiles and back up the steps. Halfway up, she turned to wave as I blew out the lamp on the table and cracked the front door open, revealing the shrouded glimmer of street lamps. I lit the small lantern that Georgy kept for me to take on my nightly walks. Then I looked up at my daughter, winked, and put my finger to my lips. The child reciprocated the gesture. As the parlour clock struck midnight, I shut the door, and with the deftness of a conjurer, vanished into the sable-misted streets of London. This was my kingdom.

When I passed through the gate onto The New Road (the silliest name for a road I had ever heard), the gas lamps were little match for the pea-soup air. And truth be told, the lantern was of little consequence one way or the other. I used it for peering into alleys and doorways, but I needed no light to guide my steps. I know these streets as well as any vagabond or street-walker. Better, in some cases. As a boy I had been left with no choice.

I turned at the junction onto Cleveland Street, where I had twice lived when younger. The aroma of cheese at the corner of Goodge Street, (we had lived in rooms above the cheese monger's) was still present, and the smell of bread from the bakery opposite it hung like a heavy curtain upon the street. The Strand Union Workhouse, nine doors down to the right, was still in full vigor. Its unforgiving brick façade was worthy of *Oliver Twist*, in which I had inconspicuously used it a decade ago.

During my youth, I had become acquainted with the souls who called these streets home. They had nothing, and so it was believed cared about nothing. They were unmoved, hardened beyond all hope of redemption. Especially the women, so everyone said.

Or were they?

Places like The Magdalen Hospital provided only a part of a solution. There, the girls could count on food, a bed, and productive ways of passing the time. The true problem came after they were released. With no home waiting for them, no reference to secure a position somewhere, their reform was meaningless. The result was a return to the street.

But if reform were accompanied by a chance to begin again somewhere else, could they succeed? Soon enough, I would have the answer. Urania Cottage, a "Home" as I preferred to term it, was nearly ready. If successful, it would be the greatest social project of its kind to date. It would work. It had to work. So far, there were three girls, with room for ten more. This Home would either be the making of them or their utter undoing.

Goodge Street takes one to Chenies Street. From there a right onto Gower Street and a left onto Keppel leads to Russell Square. I was close to our old house in Doughty Street now, where Mary had died. I closed my eyes at the memory, and walked on.

Five minutes later, I was halfway down Upper Woburn Place, heading toward the Thames. *Oh, Mary. From Heaven's perch you can see it all, can't you? Of course, for you knew me better than I know myself. Even in your innocence, you would have understood and sympathized more than most. There has been so much to do to arrange it all, and you would have helped me with all of it. You were tireless, never complaining of headaches, like Catherine. You were always the one person whom could dampen my temper and free me from frustration's teeth. You were different, dependable, decisive. So much that Catherine is, and yet is not. Would that you were at my side now.*

The dome of Saint Paul's loomed mightily as I passed it. From here I could take either Cheapside or Watling. I chose Watling. A lesser man would have turned back many streets ago and sought the warmth and comfort of his own bed. But the unknown is an addiction to those who, like me, carry the burden of the knowledge of being far from ordinary. It was something I had thanked God for on more than one occasion. It had proved to be my salvation.

Like Pickwick, I am an observer of human nature. I cannot help it. My knowledge of the London streets was as unparalleled as my imagination. A walking street index in a loud waistcoat. How that knowledge had been gained was a secret known to damned few alive. And it was going to stay that way.

The foul, dank air, thick with the soot of a million chimneys and the stench of excrement from twice that number of people filled the streets. Like breath emanating from the flared nostrils of an ancient dragon, it meditated in the streets and alleyways, waiting to devour anyone fool enough to venture in. Or anyone unfortunate enough not to escape. If my mother had had her way, perhaps I would still be there, pasting labels on pots of boot blacking.

Warren's Blacking. Those words had a taste more abhorrent to me than the bottom of a street sweeper's broom. My schooling ceased, and my books were sold. I was sold – a boy of twelve – confined to drudgery on behalf of the sins of my father. When he and the family had come out of debtor's prison, I had rejoiced, for surely my father would bring me out of Warren's. But he did not; my mother was for my staying in that rat-infested den! The woman who had given me life and had taught me to read now valued six shillings a week more than the sight of her own son. How is it that women, the epitome of delicacy and grace, can be so cruel? The ones we would be rid of remain, while the ones we would die to love are spirited away.

From Watling, a left onto Queen Street leads to the Iron Bridge, which crosses the Thames into Southwark. Here I crossed and continued to walk straight. This feeds directly to Bridge Street. In the shrouded lamplight, I saw no one about.

Then, as the bells of Southwark Cathedral proclaimed one o'clock…

"Care for company, Sir?" said a girl's voice. I turned but saw no one within the scope of my lantern. *Expect the first…when the bell tolls One…*

"Miss?" I called.

"Yes, you, dearie. Come here."

I held the lantern in front of me and walked in the direction of her voice, but still could not see her. Suddenly I caught the scent of something I had not encountered since I had last been to Paris. Cigarette smoke. Then I saw a tiny pinprick of light; an orange coal floating like a drunken bee in the darkness. Yes, it was a cigarette. I walked toward it and held my lantern up.

A small, slim girl sat on a door ledge not two feet away. She looked to me to be sixteen if she was a day; dressed in a dark lilac dress with crisscrossed bands of gray silk that ran from collar to hem. Like her, the dress was no longer new, but none the less fetching. Her long, raven hair cascaded down about her shoulders from under a matching bonnet with pink and green ruching. Whore she was, but her entire appearance suggested a dab hand with a needle.

Even a girl capable of making such clothes (or of stealing them) could not make enough from needlework to live. There was only one way to do that. And as her midnight blue eyes travelled the length of my body, I wondered if the girl was salvageable. There was only one way to find out.

"Good heavens," said I, "you're so far back in that doorway I didn't even see you."

"Well, you see me now," she said, "Want company?"

I walked closer, "And your fare?"

"For you, handsome? Five shillings."

"Is that all?" I bawked, "You're very pretty; you should charge more."

She patted the cold stone and bade me sit next to her, "If that's an offer, I'm game."

I sat beside her and set the lantern down behind us in the doorway. Her head was now at an angle that afforded me a better view. What I saw nearly stopped my heart. I knew that face.

It was *her*. I swear it to Heaven, it was my Mary! An angel fallen from Paradise into the Pit. Despite her thin frame and unkempt hair, she was pretty. Her posture, straight as a boatman's oar, was that of someone who had been taught some semblance of etiquette. No, this one was not born on the streets. And her sly smile and dry humor only increased my intrigue.

"Have—have you been at the trade long?" I inquired, trying to retain my composure at the sight of her.

"Long enough to take good care of you, darling," answered the girl as she exhaled a cloud of delicious smoke. "You interested or not?"

"Yes, I do believe I am. But not in what you think. I would like to ask you some questions. I'm happy to compensate you for your time."

She cocked a sable eyebrow. "Trouble with your girl, then, dearie?"

If only she knew. But I don't think I shall tell her.

"Hardly, my pretty," said I, "but I do have a proposition for you."

"You want to talk, then?" she said.

"Yes," I answered, "Of hot baths and good meals."

The girl tossed the remnants of her cigarette onto the cobbles and shifted closer to me. Her dark waves smelled of faint lavender mixed with sweat and soot. She put her right hand on my cheek.

"You got a tub big enough for two, do you?" The girl twirled one chestnut lock of my hair. "Hmm, very soft. Lovely."

My hand shook as I led hers gently away from my head, but I did not let it go. Her breath was thick and sour with laudanum as she pressed closer.

Don't gawk at her, you daft fellow. Say something, you idiot. Anything!

"When is the last time you saw a doctor?" said I. *Charles, pull yourself together, man!*

The girl was so taken aback all she could do was blink. No doubt this was not the type of conversation she had expected, and I couldn't help but snort a small laugh. But I could sense that she was less than amused. With dogged determination to yet separate me from some of my money, her left hand opened my great coat and proceeded to glide down the buttons of the paisley velvet waistcoat beneath.

"Doctoring don't interest me," she cooed. When she reached the third button she encircled my watch chain and slid her hand back and forth along it in a daring cadence. By now her lips were close to mine. "But I can cure whatever ails you."

The wickedness of the giggle that followed left no doubt in my mind that she could, but I kept my face and voice set in a cool reserve.

"I may surprise you on that point, my child," I said.

Her smile flashed as full and bright as her eyes. "A man walking like a demon this time of night is only after one thing."

"Is that so?"

"It is. And you've found it, dearie."

As I put my hand in hers to stop the cadence, she closed the inch of space that separated us. Our lips touched. I did not return the kiss, nor did I move away. Instead, I kept my eyes open and watched her exquisite ones close. She tilted her head and leaned against my shoulder. Her arms wrapped softly around me, her hand came to rest at the nape of my neck. Being devoid of gloves, her fingers felt like the touch of death. Like Mary's lifeless hands. *Oh God…*

"You're gentle," she cooed in my ear. "I likes that."

I shivered and pulled away. Her eyes searched me with a mixture of surprise and questioning. As alluring and willing as she was, this had to stop now. I needed her to trust me. In that moment I thought I was seeing her as few men had: gentle, vulnerable, distinctly feminine.

There was something there that could be brought forward again. Redemption was still within this girl. I stroked her cheek with the back of my hand.

"This is not what I want," I whispered.

"What do you want, then?" she sang softly.

I sat back and reached into my pocket.

"Will you walk with me, my girl?" I said, handing her five shillings.

She accepted them.

"You're paying, darling. And I'm for let."

Then she pocketed her coins and took my arm with a grin from her ready stock of appropriate faces.

"Your dress is lovely," I remarked. "A fine color on you, that lilac. Did you make it?"

"Aye."

"Remarkable talent. Tell me, what do you call these crisscrossed bands of fabric?"

"Gimpe. Saw it in *Graham's*."

"An excellent magazine. Well," I said, guiding her around a pile of proof that horses had come that way, "they are superb."

She was genuinely surprised. "Thank—thank you. Are you a tailor or something?"

"No. Tell me, if you could make enough as a seamstress, would you leave this life?"

Again, her only reply was the swift blinking of her blue eyes. She turned and encircled me with her left hand. Her right was now travelling down my chest.

"I understand, darling. No need to be nervous. Here, I'll help you."

By now her busy hand had reached already my thigh. I removed it not a moment too soon.

"Help me?" I said with a swift intake of breath.

She leaned in close against my chest.

"To get your soldier to attention," she whispered, as if she feared to embarrass me. "That why you're so keen on talking? Oh darling, don't worry. Now just relax—"

Oh God, how Catherine would howl if she heard this!

I laughed so hard that tears were streaming down my cheeks by the time I staggered back against the nearby wall. The incredulous look on her face is something I will never forget. Fear of her running off before I could explain brought back my composure.

"That particular malady has yet to find me," I said as I wiped my eyes with my handkerchief. "I am not seeking your services. I simply would like to talk with you."

"You're married." she stated.

I nodded.

"I knew it," she said softly, looking down at the road and shaking her head.

"How did you know?" I asked.

"I've known coves like you afore," she continued as she looked up at me, "the ones that only want to talk are either married or green. And you ain't green."

I snickered. "Very astute."

Her brow furrowed. "Eh?"

"It means that you are very observant," I explained.

"Can't afford to be anything else," she answered with a slight shrug of her bird-like shoulders. "All right, Dandy, take me some place warm with plenty of gin and we can talk all you like."

"Dandy?" I inquired.

"Aye. With that waistcoat and them checked trousers," said she as she tugged at them playfully, "I can hardly call you by any other name."

"Would you like to know my name?" I asked with a smile.

The girl shook her head. "It's no never mind to me. Dandy will do nicely."

"You are certain?"

"It's what I said, ain't it?"

"Very well, Lilac."

"Lilac?" she asked.

"Yes," I replied, "in honour of your dress. You need not tell me your real name, as you do not know mine. It is only fair."

She laughed, "Right, Dandy. And where shall we go now?" There was a sprinkling of humor in the tone of her voice that told me she was relieved at the prospect of the company of a man not interested in bedding her.

"Are you up for a bit of a trudge?" I asked.

"Let's make for the Rookery, Dandy."

"Bottom of Tottenham Court Road?"

"Yes, that's the one. If you're up to it, that is."

"The Rookery it is, Lilac."

Ten minutes later we were near Saint Paul's. I hailed a hansom cab, and offered my hand to help her in. She glared at me as sternly as I have ever seen it done.

"Put your hand away unless it's full of coin," she said, and entered the carriage under her own ability. I followed, and she spread half of the thick wool blanket on the seat over herself as the horse began to trot, leaving me to cover myself with the remaining portion. Soon we had passed through Cheapside, Newgate and Skinner Streets, and were continuing West on High Holborn.

"Ever been in a gin palace before, Dandy?"

"Yes. But not for some time."

She shifted closer to me, "I wouldn't have taken you for an adventurer, Dandy."

"There are a great many things you don't know about me, Lilac."

Her lips curled into a devious smile, "I think I prefer it that way."

We alighted at the bottom of Tottenham Court Road. A small man with a portable range was set up in a corner near the entrance of The Rookery, selling fried fish and whelks. Just as I was about to offer to buy her a meal, she reached into her pocket. I couldn't be sure that the coins she retrieved were among the ones I had given her a short time ago, as she could very well have already earned them before our meeting. She looked up at me and seemed to read my mind.

"You just don't learn, do you, you daft fellow?" she said. "I'll buy the supper. That's my price."

"It is positively absurd for a woman to buy," I balked.

"You may think so," said she, "But I'm not beholding to no man."

"And I, my pretty bird, am not beholding to no woman."

She placed one of her small hands on my cheek.

"You are if you want me to talk to you, my pretty Dandy."

Then she strode past me inside the establishment, a plate of fried fish in hand. The shellfish monger handed me a hot, cracked, yellow bowl of whelks, and I found Lilac at the bar.

"Cheer up," said Lilac, nudging her shoulder warmly against my arm. "Be a good boy and I'll consider letting you buy me a gin. Or ten."

I followed her through the tight crowd (an expression which was accurate in more ways than one), and we took a small corner table near a small hearth that had seen better days. There were dozens of men, women and girls walking about the ornate and brightly lit palace. All ages sought refuge here in the one thing they could count on to wash their sorrows away, albeit temporarily.

"Tuck in while it's hot, Dandy," said Lilac as she picked up a piece of fish. Then she paused, hand halfway to her mouth, "Or would you care to pray first?"

I rolled my eyes and we began to dine. In the glow of the brilliant gas jets, golden gilt and mirrors, I could see that Lilac's face was dotted with small, very faint red patches, particularly around her nose and chin. Since she had nearly finished her first gin and we hadn't been seated more than two minutes, the origin of these patches was not difficult to deduce.

"Do I shock you, Dandy?" said Lilac as licked some grease off her thumb, "You're a proper little gentleman, aren't you? Perhaps we can do something about that."

Then she wiped her mouth with her hand and rose to go buy another gin. There was no trace of the gin in her walk. I watched her maneuver her way through the crowd of smoking, swearing masses until she stood at the bar. As her shoulders only passed over the bar by several inches, she raised herself on tip toe and pointed at one of the large casks behind. I squinted to see through the smoke filled room. The label read, "Samson, 1421". I saw the bartender nod his head and fulfill her request. When she turned around I saw that she held two glasses. She set one down in front of me and reclaimed her seat. Her eyes were shining like mirrors now.

"Get that down you, Dandy. Then we'll go upstairs and talk more."

"I have told you I do not want that, Lilac," said I as I set down my glass of porter with a slim glimmer of annoyance. "Good God, I would think that would be a comfort to you, girl."

"A man at my side don't necessarily mean safety," she answered between bites, her left cheek bulging with food. "Besides, maybe I don't like safety. I'll wager you're a real goer when you've had a few glasses. And forgive me but I am noticing that you ain't shying away." said Lilac as she swallowed her food. She passed her hand through my hair, and took my hand in hers.

"Odd ring for a man," said the girl. "A blue stone like that is more suited to a girl."

"It belonged to a girl," I heard myself answer.

"Where is she now?"

I could not answer. I merely looked at her. Mistaking my silence for ardor, Lilac resumed the ritual.

"I like the look of you. You have lovely eyes."

Now it was my brow's turn to furrow.

"So do you," said I. "They are like a midnight sky."

Lilac giggled and kissed my cheek. Then she began to blow in my ear.

Charles, you idiot. Keep talking...

"How old are you, Lilac, my dear?"

"Seventeen," she answered, her teeth tugging tenderly at my earlobe.

Breathe…Remember, she is not Mary…Keep talking!

"You say you like my eyes, Lilac. What about them? Their color?"

"No," she whispered.

"Their shape?"

She kissed my ear, "No."

Good God, how could any man resist this girl?

"What, then, do you like about my eyes?" I whispered.

She looked at me and brushed her lips against mine, "The longing in them."

Charles, you fool. Stop this now.

"Lilac, I—"

"What? Can't a girl want a little fun?"

"I wouldn't advise it," I said.

"Ha! You do like to pretend, don't you, Dandy? You ain't no chaperone. You came with me of your own accord."

"For the last time, I am not-"

"Well then, perhaps I'll just seek other company."

"No you won't."

No sooner had those words escaped my mouth than she slowly pulled away.

"Oh, won't I?" she said wickedly.

A man in a dark blue coat walked by. His stride gave him away before the carved chaulk pin at his lapel came into my full vision. He was a whaler. Lilac reached for her glass. From over its rim, she gave the Harpooner a glance and he approached. He surveyed her hungrily and offered his arm. She finished the contents of her glass and made to stand.

"Stay with me," I said as I seized her wrist gently. It was so slender I feared a harsher touch would break it. But Lilac wiggled from my grasp as she rose up. She took the Boatsteerer's arm, and gave me a parting glance.

"I think you'd be better off with a copy of *Fanny Hill*, darling," she chided. And so she
Left me. When they had nearly reached the door, I rose and followed. Outside, I stood and watched them walk away until her small body was swallowed up by the fog. There was a gas lamp a few paces away, so I walked under it to consult my pocket watch. It was just after 3 o'clock. The temperature had fallen, but not to the extent that would prevent the continuation of my night walk. I would still easily be home before sunrise. A hansom approached and slowed.

"Ride home, Guv'nor?" said the driver.

"No, thank you," I replied.

"Suit yourself, Sir."

He slapped the reigns and the horse clapped along its way.

"A lovely girl, to be sure, Mr. Dickens."

"Who calls me by name?" I commanded.

A young man emerged from a nearby corner. His walk and woolen coat gave him the appearance of being a sailor, and a poor one at that. He was entirely unkempt.

"That girl's got a mind of her own, don't she? Even her lover cannot control her."

"You mean Lilac?" My pulse quickened, "Lover? The man she left with?"

"No," said the young man, "Her man is a Dandy, not no seafaring man."

"You know Lilac?"

"So, that's what she calls herself now. Aye, Mr. Dickens. I know her. And you wish to know her, too. My question is why."

"To help her, of course," I quickly added.

"Of course," he answered with unveiled sarcasm; his green eyes shining. "She weren't always so head strong. Them that she hangs out with done made her what she is. You may find it more difficult that you bargained for."

"How so?"

"If he finds out you have been jawing with his girl, he'll kill you. And you won't be his first. The likes of him don't give a damn how famous you are."

"How do you know her? Why did you not wish her to see you?"

"She ain't seen me in many years," answered the sailor. "I knew her when she were just a wee thing," he said with a playful chuckle. "It's them that she keeps company with that has made her turn."

"So you said. Why are you telling me this?"

His face became solemn as he stepped closer to me. "Save her, Mr. Dickens. Save her from herself. Her father would wish it. He loved her so. Were he alive today, he'd die of shock to know his daughter was a heartless whore."

"My dear boy," I said, "I do intend to save Lilac. But she must come willingly."

"Yes, I know. You've got a place where you send the girls. A little house."

I was shocked, "How?"

"Oh, now don't be so surprised, Mr. Dickens," he said with a wink, "You of all men should know how fast word travels in the underworld. But I will make certain it don't reach those what would harm her if they knew."

"Thank you, Mister...?"

"Matthew," he answered. "I will follow her and report to you regularly."

I reached into my pocket, "It is much appreciated."

"Put your money away," he said insistently but not devoid of pleasantry. "I do this for the girl I knew, not for you. You will see me soon. Good evening."

He offered his hand, and we shook. Then, he walked in the direction Lilac had gone with the Harpooneer. I walked a while more, but I saw no one else I thought fit for conversation. Lilac's image and softness lingered at the forefront of my brain. My neck still burned where her cold fingers had been, and the feel of her lips were still upon mine. Though, admittedly, none of those kisses had been of any consequence to her.

But that was exactly the point! She was not a common street whore. She had breeding, talent, she could read. This one could be saved. Like Matthew, I resolved to keep an eye on Lilac, and made up my mind to talk to her again and again, if necessary, until she relented.

The girl really is beautiful.
You mean she looks like me.
That is not what I said, Mary.
But it is what you were thinking.
Nonsense. I was referring to her life, not her appearance.
Of course you were.
The girl bears her fate bravely. If she resembles anyone, it would be Nancy.
Nancy is not real.
The hell she is not, I created her. I willed her into existence.
Only on paper. And then you killed her.
Correction, Bill Sikes killed her. Nancy had to die.
Like Little Nell?
Yes. To prove the point.
Even you cannot resurrect her…or me…
"No!"

It took me a moment to realize that I had cried out. I looked about me and realized that I was in Cleveland Street again. A few children were huddled in at near the entrance to the Strand Union Workhouse. They didn't even look up when I had cried out, instead remaining in their silent world that stunk of stale sewage. It was difficult to believe that the rags that covered them were ever anything that had resembled clothing. One of them, (a boy I think — though it was difficult to tell that they were human let alone their sex) stretched out a grimy, withered left hand. The last two fingers had been cut clean off. Its head then followed the direction of his hand; the left side of his jaw was in an advanced stage of putrification. His eyes were like those of a corpse, with no trace of habitation. I fumbled into my pocket, placed a few coins in the mangled paw before me, pulled the coarse wool of my collar up a bit more, and walked on.

Enough! Why shouldn't Lilac live? She - they deserve to begin again if they are willing to work for it.

I envisioned the girls at Urania; clean, safe, the brightly colored fabric of their dresses (I had been insistent upon that point) danced about them as they went about their daily duties. I envisioned them asleep in warm, clean beds. I envisioned them in the bloom of Springtime, tending their small flower gardens. As long as I was running things, reform would not be drudgery. If it weren't, it would yield a greater harvest, and Urania Cottage, I felt certain, was equipped to prove it. Society would need time to understand this. The girls themselves who would live there would need time to understand this. But, as I had written to Miss Coutts, "Never mind society". And I had meant it. True, it was her money that funded this project, though it had not been easy to get her to agree to some of my terms. I asked her to not even see the house until it was decorated. It was the penance I used for all of the meetings she conveniently forgot about; her mind more on her beloved old Duke of Wellington than the task at hand.

By the time I turned left onto Portland Place, the sun had nearly risen. I would keep my promise to Katey, and be home in more than enough time for breakfast.

CHAPTER III

WHEREIN RUBY'S SHARP EYE AND
RESOLVE ARE DISPLAYED, ALONG WITH
ANOTHER ENCOUNTER WITH THE DANDY.

The sound of glass breaking and laughter from a nearby room broke tempo with the man who now lay on top of me, heaving as if this were a race and his very life depended on finishing. He came fiercely, sweat soaking the tips of his blonde hair. In an instant, he rolled off me, panting, and padded along the darkened, creaking floorboards to his coat, which hung on the bedpost. Even in nothing but his trousers, his strut was that of a plumped peacock.

"Not the best I've ever had, but you'll do, darling." He said as he threw two shillings on the bed. "Ta."

I sat up and grabbed his arm. "I told you five."

A snort was his only reply as he put on his shirt.

"I said five," I repeated as I got off the bed.

"It's more than that fuck was worth and you know it. On your way, Cockpinch; there's a good girl."

This bloke fancied himself the biggest toad in the puddle. My hand slid toward the pocket where I kept my scissors, but stopped. If I played to his pompous nature, I could make this night an even better success. I'd soon trim his feathers for him, and the means was hanging on the bedpost: his darling blue coat. He had taken great pains to hang it up properly before laying into me. I lifted one sleeve and ran my hand down the length of it. The garment was excellently tailored. Pa would have said so.

"It's a lovely coat, Sir."

"Put that down, girl!" he said as he turned, seeing that I had removed it from the post.

"But I was only going to help you put it on," I cooed. "Oh please, Sir. You look positively dashing in it. Took my breath away, you did."

He allowed me to help him slip into his dark azure lover. I fingered the hand carved whalebone buttons and then knelt slowly, running my hands down his legs until I reached his feet.

"Such a fine figure of a man," I sang. "Help you with your shoes, Sir?"

He grinned like a cat and sat on the edge of the bed.

"Well, aren't you the little maid?" he stated.

"Only trying to make nice," I answered, putting his shoes on, "And I do hope you'll forgive my impertinence. You are a master harpooner, after all. Five shillings was far too much to ask of a man of such obvious, um, aim?"

He cupped my chin. "Too bad for you my ship sails in a few hours, Pussy. I'd love to give you a chance earn the other three shillings."

He pulled me in for a rough kiss and I clenched his thighs tightly. No sooner had he done this, than he broke the kiss abruptly and pushed me away.

"Pass us the chamber pot, girl."

I did so and he stood.

"Pumping bilges, Sir?" I joked as I pulled my bodice back up and fastened it. I was surprised he had lasted that long; from the whiskey on his breath I had wagered his bilges were fit to overflow. He laughed rather heartily at that. I put my bonnet on and made for the door. Then I turned around when I reached it and clicked my heels together like a soldier and stood ramrod straight.

"Permission to leave the ship, Sir?" I said, lowering my voice to sound like a boy.

"Aye, my little bilge cat," he answered, still pissing, his back turned to me.

I smirked and knuckled the side of my forehead like I had seen some sailors do once when they saluted an officer. His stream was still hitting the pot as I slipped out of the room, his wallet tucked safely in my corset. Then I ran as if Old Scratch himself were after me, and headed for home.

Thankfully, no one else was home yet, and I was thankful for the quiet. The chill in the early morning air made me thankful that Mousie had laid a fire the previous night. I lit the fire and the lamp. Their light danced over my small room, illuminating the fashion illustrations from *Godey's* and *Grahams* that I had pasted on my walls. The mirrors, fabrics and furs strewn about my room gave it the look of an exotic harem. It was meant to provide inspiration; to make the men hard. But now the room mocked me; it was a cage.

I fingered the ribbon on the brown bonnet on my work table. It was fetching. Top would like it. In the beginning it had been all flattery and gifts. But now, my face, my name, I, did not matter. I was a vessel in doll's clothes. A hole to play in. Perhaps

I was not so different than those pretty girls in the fashion drawings after all?

I started thinking about the Dandy I had drunk with last night. I liked the look of him. He had named me Lilac. It was just as well, I never give my real name to any man. That was one of Top's rules. I peeled out of my lilac dress and hung it carefully on its peg, and threw my petticoats down in the nearby basket. *I'll have Mousie wash these.*

The Harpooner's wallet slid easily out of my corset, and I cried out upon seeing its contents. A five pound note! I quickly changed into a plain brown dress and went to the washstand. The mirror showed me that I had taken too much laudanum again last night. There was also a slight throb in my head. But all I wanted was sleep, and laudanum was the only way to get it. Normally Mousie or Collette tended to my requests. But, they were out, confound them both. I opened the cupboard and took the gin bottle from the third shelf on the left. Some hot water from the hob into a pewter noggin, a bit of gin and a few drops of laudanum, and I'd be set to right in no time.

I settled into bed and drew the quilts up close. I took long sips of the tonic, and soon it caressed me inside with delicious silken strokes. A truer love I never had, not even Top. Soon sleep came for me, banishing the strange man from my mind.

I was sitting next to my father. The sun shone through the open window. The red ribbon in my hair flickered on my cheek against the warm breeze.

"Pa, tell me a story."

"Which one, Ruby?" he said as he looked up from the table. He was chalking a new waistcoat out of black velvet.

"Any one."

"Let's make one up. One day there was—"

I looked up at him, "No, Pa. Once upon a time — Ow!"

"My dear, you need to pay better attention."

I nodded, my finger in my mouth. It didn't take long for the bleeding to stop, and I asked him to begin the story.

"Very well. Once upon a time," he paused, signaling me to continue.

"A fairie sat on the branch of a tree," I came out with all at once.

Pa put down his chalk and picked up the scissors. The tape measure around his neck, browned with age and frayed at the ends, had belonged to his Pa. I always wondered how he always managed to only cut the cloth and never his tape.

"What kind of tree?" he asked, looking at me over the top of his spectacles.

"An oak tree, of course." I answered, nearly finished with the hem on the trouser leg.

His lips molded into a smile. "Of course. Is it night?"

"Yes."

"And is she a good fairie?"

"Yes. She helps people."

"All the time?"

"No, only when they are good."

"Ruby," I heard a voice call my Christian name.

"Pa?" I whispered as he began to fade from my laudanum—induced dream.

"Ruby, my lamb. Open your eyes," it said. There was only one man allowed to call me by my true name. I opened my eyes and saw Top sitting on the bed next to me. He smiled and removed the top hat of peacock blue velvet from which he took his name. He was a handsome fellow, with green eyes and his hair the color of weak coffee with a few drops of milk. I was the sugar that filled his cup. He sat there and looked down at me as a puppy to its mistress. He adored me. He took care of me. And secretly, I despised him for it.

In many ways, Top was as a naive child. In his eyes, I could do no wrong. Not once in all these years had he ever scolded or spoken to me harshly. True, he was also a good lover. Very good, in fact. But he had been easily conquered, and I had lately begun to grow increasingly bored.

"Where were you last night?" he asked kindly.

"You know I like to walk," I answered as I yawned and stretched.

"You should not go out at night alone, my love," said Top.

"Well, no one was here to keep me company," I pouted, looking up at him with sad, playful eyes.

"My poor darling," Top said apologetically as he leaned down and kissed me. "I had important business to attend to."

"It's always business," I sighed as I sat up.

"You must not leave me."

"I didn't leave you, Top. I went for a walk."

"You used to be afraid to go out into the streets. Remember how you came to be here with me."

"Yes," I said as I rolled my eyes, "I have not forgotten."

"I cared for you. I schooled you. I find only the best men for you. And they give you pretty things," he said musically as he gestured around the room.

"Top," I said, taking his face in my hands, "You take good care of me. Of course I like it here, you silly fellow."

"You are the only thing that matters to me, Ruby," he whispered with emotion as he laid his head on my breast.

"I know," I said kindly as I wrapped my arms around him and kissed his hair, "You have helped me not be afraid of going out. So, I went out. And now I am home, and I am fine!"

"But something could happen-" he said as he looked up at me.

"Oh for God's sake, Top," I said as I broke the embrace and walked to my dressing table, "Do you want to keep me locked up?"

"I only want to protect you."

"I can protect myself. Now either change the subject or get out. And where are Mousie and Collette? Honestly, can't you just sack them and get some decent help?"

"I brought you a present."

I spun around on my stool. "Present?"

"To apologize for my absence last night."

I rose and walked back over to him as he still sat on the edge of my bed. He guided me to his lap and reached into his pocket. In his hand was a turquoise pendant on a gold chain.

"It isn't my color," I said, unamused, and pouted.

He chuckled. "It's the meaning of the color— the color of a special flower."

"Which one?"

"Forget Me Not."

I giggled and let Top fasten the necklace around my neck. He kissed my neck, and did not stop there. He knew what I liked, and I cooed as that delicious tingling, dripping heat began to stir inside me. He lay me on the bed, then lowered himself on top of me.

"You are pleased?" he whispered slyly.

"More than I was," I said, then kissed him back.

"Mmmm. Tell me how I can please my girl more?"

"Worship me," I ordered, as I opened my legs underneath him.

*****

The afternoon had turned to night by the time I walked out of Urania and into the waiting carriage. If Mrs. Holdsworth thought she would run the home according to her own whims, she was dreaming wide awake. Our conversation had taken longer than I had planned. As a result, I had not worked as much on the latest installment of *Dombey* as I had wanted.

Confound that obstinate dragon; who was she to question my directions? If the schedule I had drawn up stated that everyone rises at seven o'clock in the morning, even on washday, then by God it had better be so. I had directed her to participate in the washing, not just dictate to the girls. Apparently rising early was not to her liking. Today she looked at me, sulky and grum, and declared that she couldn't do it.

Balderdash! I had half a mind to drag her down to the Thames to see the mudlarks. Perhaps the sight of withered old women in rags with backs bent from years of toil, clothes encrusted with muck, and raw, cracked skin on their hands from the frigid, putrid river would loosen the scales from her eyes. It was always something with that woman.

Her face had shown a glint of disdain weeks earlier when I marked which prayers she was to use from the prayer book. I wish I could have drawn her face and showed it to Miss Coutts! But my four girls, Julia, Rosina, Mary Anne, and Frances, already ensconced within Urania Cottage, all looked well. Still, the rules for the Holdsworth woman were the same for the rest. I would brook no slackness; they would obey and work together, or they would leave and make way for more deserving women. As Mr. Brownlow had said to Oliver Twist, "You need not be afraid of my deserting you, unless you give me cause."

Despite the ordeal, the drama of it all had been a welcome respite. The girl in the lilac dress still intrigued me. Truthfully, I had thought of little else since. She was perfect for the Home. I wanted to see her again. I wanted to know her. Not in the Biblical sense, of course. But dear God, she was among the most beautiful young girls I had ever seen, and I'll not deny it.

There is often a fire burning inside these street girls, a flame that emanates from them and is as tactile as flesh. Sometimes it emanates pain, like the ones in prison. Others emote desperation, like a great many of the flower girls, who sell a damn sight more than flowers to survive. But the one thing that I always looked for was courage, and the girl I had met last night was consumed with it. Lilac wanted to live, and the flame fanning within her was different. It did not burn to the bone like the passion that had possessed me when I courted the vixen Maria Beadnell all those years ago. Far from it. This girl was a whore, and probably a thief like most of my Urania girls. But put Lilac in the same room as Maria with a roomful of callers, and by charm alone, Lilac would be the victor. I would have given half my fortune to see it.

As the wheels rolled on the frozen cobbles toward home, I thought more about that first moment when Lilac kissed me. It meant nothing to her; merely the means to get what she wanted. But I could not forget the image of those exquisite eyes closing as she rested her head on my shoulder. There was a grace there under that stern and cocksure facade. Had she ever loved? Who was he? Did he love her, or had he broken her heart? Were they lovers? Did she envision him when she was with men, or when she had kissed me?

The carriage rounded a corner a too fast for my liking on a slick road, and sent me sliding down the seat from the right corner to the left. It jarred me from my thoughts, and I banged with my cane against the top of the carriage.

"Sorry, Mr. D." I heard the coachman holler. "Dead dog in the road, Sir."

I pulled my collar up closer as the carriage rounded the corner, and looked out the window. Then I realized I had been holding my breath. I exhaled, and watched the mist form on the dirt-splattered glass. The air was indeed cold tonight. But Lilac's charms had been colder. She had bit my soul more savagely than a January frost with her passionate indifference.

As with the other girls at Urania, her life was a tomb of vice and regret. Lilac had thought to seduce me, but it was I who would seduce her. But what I had to offer her was even more desirable, something she had forgotten. It was the most desirable object in the world, and what my dear Mary had embodied and perfected.

Virtue.

Light and dark are equal parts; like the sides of coin. What people fail to realize is that light can be just as disorienting as darkness. One is as irresistible as the other. Kindness can bruise the soul far worse than blows, especially when it is unexpected. Getting this girl to say yes to Urania would roll the stone away. And then, like Lazarus from the tomb, I would resurrect her.

At length I found myself retracing my steps of the previous nights across Southwark Bridge. I saw a girl leaning against a lamp post, gazing down into the Thames. Her wide bonnet shrouded her face in shadow – this being the curse of that particular fashion. Though she had changed her lilac dress for one of a faded blue, I knew her. The garment possessed her slender form like a second skin. Her black hair framed her shoulders the way it had when I had watched at the bar of The Rookery. I would know her anywhere. Yes, it was Lilac.

The lamplight allowed me to see that her dress was twice turned. Women often turn clothes inside out and then turn them again for even wear. But such was Lilac's ability with a needle that only a keen eye would have noticed it. This girl was clever. Of course, I wanted to help her to find a new life. She would do so well at Urania, I knew. And I felt certain if she would confide in me, she would make a wonderful story. It could be such an admirable arrangement for the both of us. But seeing her on the bridge at night, staring at the Thames, worried me, and with reason.

"It's cold over the river at night, Lilac," said I.

"Used to it," the expression on her face was that of indifference. She exhaled one last puff of smoke and cast the remains of her cigarette to a cobbled grave as she turned to me, "You back again?" she asked, as if she half expected me.

I shrugged, "Fanny didn't do it for me, I'm afraid."

Lilac turned her back to the Thames and leaned against the lamppost a pace away to her right.

"You're a strange one and no mistake, Dandy," she said.

"You're far from the first to think that. Have you any other engagements this evening, Lilac?"

"I don't work for you, darling," replied the girl, "Not your business."

"On the contrary," said I, procuring coin from my pocket, "it is my business."

She raised her eyebrows playfully. "Still want to chat, do you?"

I showed her five shillings on my gloved palm. "I promised to pay you for your time, did I not?"

She held out her hand and took them. Then she looked up at me.

"How do I know you ain't just a Peeler in fop's clothing? They catch us like that sometimes."

"I defy any Peeler to have a better dress sense than myself. Let us go somewhere and talk, and I shall explain everything, I promise."

As a token gesture, I handed her another five shillings. To my surprise, Lilac did not take the coins this time. Instead, she took a step away from me.

"What makes you think I'll accept?" she asked warily.

A hansom was approaching, and I flagged it down.

"Get in," I said.

Lilac stood there, shoulders straight, and glared at me.

"I do not like to repeat myself, girl. Get in."

"Fuck you," she spat, "as if you could order me about!"

"I have paid your fare; your time is now mine. You like money, and here it is. Now get in."

She smacked my hand, and confined the coins to Father Thames.

"To hell with your goddamned lolly! No man orders me!" she exclaimed as she turned to leave.

Before I knew what I was doing, my hand was around her forearm and I deposited her inside the cab. I looked down at Lilac, and she turned away from me.

"I could scream for the Peelers, you know."

"Scream away, Lilac. They know me."

For the first time, I saw fear in her hard eyes.

"Who are you?" she asked.

"I thought you told me you were not interested in my name."

"Well, I am now."

"A friend," I replied, "Someone who has the power to help you."

Her only reply was a snort.

"Would you like to know where we are going?" I asked as I covered us both with the blanket.

"No," was her monotone response. Her chest was heaving nervously, and her jaw was set hard. I knew I had grossly embarrassed her. But she had left me with no choice. The ride would give me time to smooth her feathers.

"We shall go wherever you like, Lilac," I responded.

The girl was silent for many minutes before she spoke again.

"Fine. Back to the Rookery, then."

"As you wish," I said as I pointed up to the small door above our heads, "Open the door up there and tell the driver."

Lilac did so, then turned her gaze straight ahead. Even with the motion of the cab as we travelled,

Lilac remained as a statue, her face devoid of emotion. The angle of her chin gave the illusion of the figurehead of some dark, solemn ship that had wandered the blackest oceans, forever seeking a port it is destined never to find.

"You've got more bite in you than I thought, Dandy," she remarked as she watched the street pass by us.

"Indeed I do," I answered. I smiled devilishly and leaned close to her ear, "And this time, Lilac, I am buying the supper."

CHAPTER IV

BACK AT THE ROOKERY, WHERE SECRETS ARE NEARLY BETRAYED

Once again, we alighted at The Rookery. The gilt glistened as to mock the emotion which shares its pronunciation. In all its unrepentant splendour, it was glorious. I ordered two gins and some fried fish, since I knew it was to Lilac's liking. We sat where we had during our first meeting. A woman was lustily singing out in song a few tables down. The crowd around her, mostly drunken men, were cheering and singing. Lilac joined in with full voice on the chorus:

"Cherry ripe, ripe I cry. Full and fair ones, come and buy!"

The way she looked at me as she sang sent my blood rushing. A wave of annoyance surged through me. I wanted to flee this den. I wanted to take her with me. I wanted—

Get out of here!

"I did not pay you to sing, Lilac. Let us finish and go somewhere quiet to discuss things."

"Oh I forgot," responded Lilac in that mocking tone she used so deftly. "You don't like to have fun, do you? You really ain't interested in me, Dandy?" asked my fascinating companion.

"No."

"Liar."

"I beg your pardon, young lady?" I snapped.

The girl stood up abruptly, kicking her chair back with her tiny foot. She rushed at me, straddled my lap, and leaned in close to me. Her hands caressed my hair and face as she spoke, the look of lust in her eyes.

"You sanctimonious prat. You like to pretend, don't you? Pretend that you're a Gentleman. Pretend that you're respectable. But secretly, you'd love to be like us, wouldn't you? Unrespectable, unrepentant. Free. You're itching, aching to let go, aren't you? Aye, that's your temptation, ain't it? You'd bask in it, given half the chance."

Her words were a sharp as if she had struck me. I did not move. I dared not move. Then she kissed me, full on and with a power I would not have believed her small frame to possess. She squeezed my seat with her thighs, and looked at me in triumph.

"Let's see how brave you really are, my little Gent," said Lilac as she slid off my thighs and took my hand in hers. As she led me upstairs, I did not resist her.

*****

I seized his hand. He did not protest.

The gaslights, still bright (for they are never turned off here), revealed a bacchanalia at full gallop. Men, drunk with drink and desire, were atop and underneath an array of women of varying ages, sizes, and colors. Silks, taffetas and cottons, stained with brandy, gin, madeira and the spending of countless customers lay on velvet chaises, tables and floors. It was a smoky, sweating, stinking, sticky, colorful wash of selfishness and lust.

Never releasing his hand, I led Dandy to a corner chaise. It amused me to regard him as he observed the scene. His bright eyes missed nothing. They consumed that room as surely and as deeply as a tankard of porter. Sure that I would conquer him, I wrapped my arms around the back of his neck and drew his lips to mine. Though he did not resist, it did not seem to faze him.

Until his arms tightened around me.

"Here, give me a go, Pussy."

We broke the kiss to find another man eyeing me. He was taller and with a much broader build than Dandy's. His red beard framed an eagle-like face with very bloodshot blue eyes. He seized the arm of the near unconscious girl at his feet. Her once green silk dress was torn off her shoulders and stained all the colors of that make up the rainbow of debauchery.

"Share and share alike, Mate," said the man as he practically tossed the girl to Dandy, "this one's nice and tight. Try her and I'll let you know how yours is."

The fire-haired man reached for me and began to pull at my dress. Dandy released the girl (she landed on the chaise, though past caring), and pulled me from my assailant. The drunkard dealt him a heavy blow across the face, but Dandy gave as good as he got. He landed a blow to the man's jaw that took the wind from his sails long enough for me to use my knee where it counted. The pig landed in a pool of his own puke. Then we both dashed out of the chamber and into the passage.

"Blimey, now that was fun," I said, breathless.

"Fun?" asked Dandy, hands on his thighs as he tried to control his own panting. "Fun?"

"Aye. You handle your fives well, I must say. Let's go back in and do it again."

He looked at me as if my head sat upon my neck the wrong way, "Are you mad, girl?"

"Maybe. But don't tell me you didn't enjoy that as well. Perhaps I shall go back in there without you."

Dandy took my arm, "Child, I forbid it."

I shot him a threatening glance, "Mark me, Dandy, I keep company with whom I choose."

"And your point?"

"Simple. I can go with them or you. It don't make no never mind to me."

"And you prefer their kind over me — a man who will not hurt you?"

I shook my arm out of his grasp, "Stow the pious bullshit. You want something from me. If you're too much of a coward to say it, then yes, I prefer the likes of they."

"Why?"

"Because at least they're honest enough to admit they want to fuck me."

Something in his eyes changed. In a flash, he seized both my shoulders and pinned me to the wall. He leaned his face down and kissed me full on.

"That's more like it," I panted when he broke the kiss.

"Do not toy with me¸" he growled less than an inch from my lips, "for I tolerate it from no woman. If you take me for some wretched little choir boy, you are gravely mistaken."

"Prove it," I taunted in a low whisper.

He made to kiss me again, but instead trailed his lips to my cheek.

"Show me where you live," he rumbled harshly in my ear.

"No."

"I want to tell you the truth, Lilac."

"What truth?" I asked.

He passed a hand gently across my cheek, "You deserve better. You are above this, all of it."

"What are you playing at? Out to save the little whore, are you?" I said as I narrowed my eyes at him.

"Are you interested?"

"A lofty ambition, to be sure. It could cost you dearly."

His gaze was hypnotic.

"Name your price, woman."

*****

It was pouring with rain when I found us a room in Goodge Street. We settled in near the fire, and she warmed some gin for us. I further requested lemon, sugar and nutmeg at the very least be brought as well, that I could make punch. It was not long before we were both more than three sheets to the wind…

"You can't be serious," she giggled, taking another sip.

"I am perfectly serious. If I could have married her, I would have."

"Little Red Riding Hood?"

"She was my first love. Aye, I still love her. A wife like that? Why, her fame is nearly equal to mine."

"Is that right? And are you somebody, Sir?" asked Lilac, adding a mocking curtsey.

"As a matter of fact, dear girl, my name is umph!"

She never finished that curtsey, and fell into my arms, laughing. Her long hair splayed around her face, framing it in a mahogany glow. The glint of the gin palace danced in her eyes. She looked so much like...*No! Stop thinking of her.* But already I could feel the wine dancing its way to my brain, and recalled a poem.

> "Her cheeks like the dawn of day,
> And her bosom white as the hawthorn buds
> That ope in the month of May."

"Longfellow. Nice," said Lilac. "But you forgot the part about fairy-flax. I am a Faerie, you know."

"You are indeed, my dear."

As if she read my thoughts, she turned to look up at me.

"Want to kiss me, don't you?"

"Yes, Mary. I want to kiss you."

"Who's Mary?"

My heart quickened.

"I—I didn't say Mary."

"Yes you did, Dandy."

"I'm not that drunk yet, Lilac. I know your name."

She giggled, "You are drunk, and you're completely mad. I like you."

She snuggled closer to my chest and curled her legs up as a baby ready for sleep. Then, she drifted off to sleep on gin's warming tide. The last thing I remember was her soft, magnificent cooing against my neck as it carried me to an equally blissful sleep.

I did not kiss her.

*****

I could feel the smile on my face when I awoke. Dandy was still asleep. The laudanum I used on the gin had not failed me. I eased myself out of his embrace and sat up. My back was sore from the awkward position in which I had slept, and as I stretched I regarded his face. His shoulder-length hair of a dark chestnut and clean-shaven face did give him an almost feminine air. With the dexterity of a pickpocket (which Top had taught me), I reached into his waistcoat. One pocket had a watch. The other held a tiny golden box, which bore the initials *C. D.* I opened it and found a compass inside. Attached to the thick, gold chain that held the watch was a small pendant with dark and light green swirls. It was a stone of some kind, and the shape reminded me of something like a knight's shield from story books I had seen as a child. I turned it over and read the inscription:

From
C. D.
To
M. S. H.
1835

With a sly smile, I began to carefully undress him. I deposited his clothes in a neatly folded bundle on the bed, and made up the fire. Then I returned to the bed and sat upon his clothes.

Dandy soon stirred. He made to stand, and then realized he was naked.

"What the—?"

"Morning, Dandy," said I as I smiled and winked at him.

He turned his head wildly in all directions, trying to find his clothes. The bed was within arm's reach. He seized the blanket and snatched it to cover himself with.

"Have you gone daft, Child?" he exclaimed, "Give me my clothes at once!"

"You are free to leave at any time, my dear Sir. A sailor I once knew got into your position one night. He was obliged to borrow one of the girl's dresses to get back to his ship on time. Course his mates never let him live it down. If you're inclined to borrow mine, though, it will cost you, with interest."

He sat up ramrod straight. His thin, muscled legs jut straight out from the blanket that covered his manhood. He shivered and drew the fabric closer around his body.

"And now that I have your undivided attention," I continued in the most angelic voice I could summon, "kindly tell me just what the fuck you want of me?"

"I believe the more pressing question at present is what you want of me," he said quietly.

I reached into my reticule and took out my scissors. Smiling, I rose from my chair and knelt next to him.

"Cold?" I asked.

"Yes," he answered.

"Perhaps I can make you warm again," I said in a husky whisper.

He dared not move as I perched myself on his outstretched thighs. I traced his face gently with the scissors, moving even down his chest. His magnificent eyes never left mine. Half full of terror, half of excitement, they questioned me and begged of me all at once. When I reached his manhood, the tremble of his breath gave birth to a loud gasp when my scissors sliced the morning air.

"Now you know how I feel sometimes," I said, leaning in less than an inch from his lips.

His eyes closed as he let out a shuddered sigh of relief.

"What must I do to earn back my clothes?" he whispered.

"Explain yourself," I said, "now, if you want to leave this room intact."

Dandy licked his lips and swallowed hard.

"I was serious about what I said last night."

"What was you serious about?"

"That you deserve better."

I snorted and rose. "Back to that again, are we? Christ."

"I would not say such things if I could not act upon them, Lilac."

I turned to face him and held out the scissors in front of me as a lady would her closed fan.

"What in hell are you playing at, Dandy?"

He stood, his bare feet agitated by the cold bare boards beneath them.

"I am not playing at all," said my captive as he adjusted the blanket, "There is a place, a Home, that will be opening soon for girls like you who deserve a second chance. I cannot help but think you would do very well there. Those are the facts."

"Shit, I knew it. A reform house," I said, and went to poke the fire.

"No," insisted the naked Dandy as he followed me, "It is a house where you would not be judged, and where could erase the past."

"So, you're a wizard, too, eh?" I said as I downed the dregs of the gin we had drunk last night.

"Some have called me that," he said as he smiled. I could see his teeth were chattering slightly. "Besides, I grow tired of meeting you in the dark, in secret. Let me take you for a real supper in a more respectable place."

"Where?"

"Do you know Russell Square?"

I thought for a moment. "I do."

"Good. Be there tomorrow at ten o'clock. I shall be in a hansom at the entrance to Monmouth Street, near the British Museum. Let me take you for a decent breakfast. It will be your turn to ask the questions, my dear. Now how does that sound?"

"But I—"

No sooner had these words dripped from my maw than this strange man put his hands on my shoulders. He regarded me with a powerful tenderness that made me shudder.

"Say you will meet me there. Please. I—I want very badly to tell you things. Things you need to hear. You are a lovely girl who deserves a lovely breakfast, and answers to whatever questions you have for me."

The look in his eyes—that gentle intensity. I had only ever seen that in one other man. It frightened me; it gave me pause. I couldn't resist.

"Fine," I heard myself say. "Ten o'clock tomorrow it is, then."

I stood up on the bed and gestured to his clothes. Dandy kissed my forehead exuberantly, and dressed himself with the speed most men use to take their clothes off.

"You will not regret this, Lilac," he said, as he finished the last button on his waistcoat.

"I'll believe that when it's proved to me."

CHAPTER V

A MOST UNPLEASANT BREAKFAST.

I put my coffee cup down and smiled. The slips of paper that I found underneath my plate were exceptionally good today. The children liked to leave poems and drawings for me. It this was their way of keeping themselves in my mind when my characters had me kidnapped. It isn't that I was ignoring them intentionally, just that when my characters demanded attention, all else came second. The children had since finished and were back in the nursery with their Aunt Georgie. That left Kate and myself at table.

"Kate, look at this one. Mamie does have a flair, I declare!"

She smiled as she looked at the paper I held out. "Yes, Charles."

I took a last sip of coffee.

"You don't seem very interested, Kate."

She dabbed a bit of toast into her egg.

"I am," she answered. "but it's just that I have much on my mind today."

"The creative stimulation of your children is of no value to you, I see? I've no time for your moods today, Kate. It's time I was in the study."

"*Dombey & Son*?" she asked.

"That's right. There's another installment due soon. And there's much going on at Urania. I may have found another girl. She'll do very well there, I am sure of it. Kate? Are you listening?"

Kate didn't seem to hear me, and continued to stare into her boiled egg.

"I don't think you'll find Mr. Dombey in there, Kate," I mused, hoping she would smile. But she did not smile. "Kate?"

Still, she did not look up. My hand clenched around my napkin. Kate always liked childish games, but I had no time for it.

"Kate!"

She looked up at me, "Charles, please. My head aches so." Her response was distant. Her eyelids were heavier than usual today, and they seemed slightly swollen. Another of her frequent headaches, no doubt. Why did she always get this way when she was expecting a child?

"I'm sorry that the welfare of these poor girls is such a bore for you. No doubt you've much more important things to tend to, like headaches. And I must say that I think I'm coming down with one, too."

"Charles, I—"

"Get some rest," I said curtly, "you're obviously not well today. Thank Heaven one of us is responsible enough to keep a roof over the heads of this endless brood." Then I hurried out, leaving Kate to breakfast alone. If she wanted to act like a child, I would treat her as one.

I stormed through my study door, slammed it behind me, and ran my hand through my hair. More pressing matters were at hand than her contemptible moods. Last night I could find no trace of that girl I was still searching for. Lilac—whatever her name was, every ounce of instinct screamed worry, but there was nothing I could do except keep looking.

For now, work must come first. So I sat down at my desk, which was bathed in the warm morning sunlight. I bid Mr. Paul Dombey welcome as he appeared, and I allowed him to take command. Gradually, thoughts of girls in lilac and wives with headaches were scratched away by the sound of my pen.

CHAPTER VI

UNEXPECTED ENCOUNTERS.

"Collette! I need my red dress pressed. The red fan front bodice. Now!"

I hung up my bonnet and shawl, and look about the parlor. No one answered my call.

"Collette? Mousie? Look alive!" I shouted.

Still nothing. The fire in the grate was sputtering as if it had not been tended in some time. I walked over and revived it with the poker, and added some coal from the scuttle.

"So I am a charwoman now, eh? If I get coal dust on this dress, Collette, Top will have your hide! It's time for my tea. And be certain we have wine. I just may have a Gentleman caller this evening."

There was no response from any nearby chamber. I sighed in annoyance and walked down the passage and into the kitchen. A pot was boiling over on the hob, and I procured a towel from the table and moved it. The pot ceased its vomiting of foam, but not before it extinguished what little coal was still burning. Dark, smoky liquid slopped out of the grate and onto my foot.

"Shit!" I exclaimed, as I hopped for a moment on one foot. I sat at the table and dabbed at my boot with a towel. All the tea things were on their usual silver tray (the china with hand-painted fruit had been a gift from Top). The tin of Twining's was overturned, its dark contents scattered upon the tray.

"Clumsy old woman," I remarked as I rolled my eyes. "I'll make the fucking tea myself."

With great annoyance, I threw the towel back on the table and looked over at the coal scuttles. They were both empty.

"Christ," I said through a clenched jaw as I rose and picked up one of the scuttles. I walked to the coal bin, opened it, and prepared to reach in with the shovel.

That's when I saw her. Or rather, her head, for she was buried to her ears in the coal. A pair of dead, half-closed eyes greeted me. Blood still trickled down through a crack in her old skull, marrying the coal below. Her brains had so soaked into her white hair that one was now indistinguishable from the other.

Top! Oh God, what have you done?

I dropped the scuttle and to the sink and jerked the pump like a madwoman. The water I threw on my face did nothing to calm me, though.

Top is a murderer? Oh please, no! I—I need time to think...

"He done it," said Mousie. I looked about, but did not see her.

"Mousie?"

"He done it," she repeated. I followed the sound of her voice. She was under the sink. The crevice in which she had hid was so small even I could not have fit. But she slid her body out with ease.

"He done it," said Mousie for a third time.

"Top?"

She drew a knife from her pocket. Her eyes were wild. I backed away.

"We was going to leave here, her and me. Tonight. Sick of waiting on the likes of you. Sick of eating scraps that you didn't want. She stole from your room; found that wallet you hid from Top. He come home early and found her rummaging. She told him all she thought of you, and he beat her to death. It's all your fault, whore. I should have left you to rot where I found you that day. It's all your fault she's dead!"

I don't remember running up the stairs. I don't remember if I closed the front door behind me as I ran. I don't remember fetching my bonnet and shawl as I left. But I must have done, because I wore them as I stopped to catch my breath near The Strand.

I attempted to slow my walking as I made my way across the street. When I reached the next set of lamps, three gentlemen passed by me, clad in evening dress, black cloaks and fine beaver top hats. A toss with each of them and I could live for a fortnight. But they paid me no heed.

By now I had turned right, toward the Thames. Then two large, blue-sleeved arms came up around my shoulders. A hand clamped down on my mouth.

"Where's my wallet, bitch!"

It was the harpooner from the other night at The Rookery. He tossed me in the alley behind him like a parcel. I landed in a pile of old empty hogsheads. One of those small wooden casks rolled over me, causing me to cry out.

"You're going to work off every bit of the money you nicked from me, you precocious slut," he said.

I managed to stand only to find the barrel of his pistol two feet from my face. I moved away from him, and soon felt the kiss of rough brick against my back.

"One squeak out of you and this ball goes in your head," growled the brute.

I spit in his face and he struck me. Then he fastened his other hand around my neck and led me toward an overturned hogshead, and bent me over it. I felt him lift my skirts. As he fumbled to undo his trousers I saw one half of a wooden stave on the ground in front of me. I prayed it was within reach. It was. I seized the stave with both hands and flung it over my head with all my strength. He drew back, screaming curses at me. The pistol fell from his hand. I grabbed it and scrambled over the hogshead and the other derelict casks toward my bag. But when I turned to leave the alley he was already on his feet, a trickle of blood running from his hair down the bridge of his now crooked nose.

I raised the pistol and fired.

It only clicked.

He grinned like the devil.

"I knew with you I didn't need to load it. Now be a good little cunt and I won't thump the life out of you."

A cry of rage escaped my lips and I hurled the useless thing straight at him. He easily ducked to avoid it, and rushed me, pinning me back up against the wall. He proceeded to strike me twice more, in my face and gut. Then I felt the back of my dress tear as it was grated like nutmeg against the brick wall as he rode me with a savagery I hadn't felt since…

Oh God, not again.

It was over quickly, and he grunted in satisfaction as he stepped back. I sank to the filthy cobbles as limp as a laundress's bundle. The bastard buttoned his trousers. I clawed my nails into the mortar of the wall and tried to stand, but I could not.

He spat upon me. Then he was gone.

Even after I found my feet, I still had to lean against the brick until my breath returned. I turned onto the street. There was a bridge nearby. Waterloo? Perhaps. What did it matter now?

The only sound was the hungry lapping of the Thames against the moss-laden stone below. Within the fog-shrouded web of the black, stinking conduit, I could scarcely make out the tall tangle of masts and rigging at the wharves. They were revealed only by the running lights and anchor lanterns. Tiny pinpricks of red, green, and white in the black fog.

I stood looking down into the liquid mass as thick as wet coal. I ached everywhere; it had not happened since I was little. The recollection made me feel as if I would puke, and I did. People shoved by me, thinking me just another drunk whore in the dim lamplight leaning over the bridge. But they shoved too hard. I swayed and clawed, but it was no use. All at once, I was upon the water.

CHAPTER VII

DICKENS LEARNS DREADFUL NEWS.

The carriage door opened. But it was not Lilac who entered. It was Matthew. And the look on his face turned my heart cold.

"What has happened?" I asked curtly.

"She was attacked. I found her in the Thames. Whether she fell or was pushed in, I know not-"

The world turned scarlet. I suddenly found my hands clenched about his coat.

"You promised to follow her! To protect her!"

Matthew seized me by my own lapels, "Am I not but a man, Sir? Will it not haunt me until the end of my days that she was hurt? Aye, mark me, it will!"

There we stayed, eyes and fists locked, for several minutes. Then Matthew sighed, and released me. I reciprocated, and reached for my brandy flask. I handed it to the young man, and waited for him to continue his account, which he did after taking a long sip. "She is alive, Mr. Dickens."

"Where?" I asked.

"Tothill Fields. Bridewell."

"Yes, I know it. Governor Tracey is a friend of mine. I shall write to him and make certain Lilac has an excellent doctor."

"That's all I needed to hear, Mr. Dickens. I shall meet you again in one week. By then I hope to have more information about her acquaintances."

"Very well, Matthew. Good day."

"And to you, Sir," said Matthew as he tipped his cap. "And one more thing."

"What is it?"

"Ruby. Her real name is Ruby. Ruby Waller." He winked, and took his leave.

Ruby? Yes, it suits her. She is a fiery little jewel!

CHAPTER VIII

RUBY WALLER'S DELIRIUM.

By now I could open my eyes. I was in a room with brick walls that I did not recognize. My body was on fire, my hair and chemise were sweat soaked.

Where the blazes am I?

The pain was wrenching, I could not stop shaking or get a deep breath. An old woman was bathing my forehead with a piece of cloth, her hands smelled of onions and soap. Her face was worn with rivers of wrinkles that spoke of a life of drudgery, and the ruffled cap on her head was as coarse as the black woolen shawl about her shoulders. She spoke, revealing a complete vacancy of teeth.

"Girl's awake, Doc."

I moved my head in the direction of her eyes. A dark brown-haired man with a short, neat beard filled my vision. His brown eyes looked down at me with stern compassion as he held a tin cup full of foul smelling liquid to my lips. As great as my thirst was, I wanted to spit it out for fear of vomiting again, and I struggled to sit up. But he held me as the woman held my mouth shut, forcing me to swallow. I could see and hear them, but I felt as if my body were somewhere else.

"The fever's got her now, Mrs. Mick. Her crisis will be violent. Watch her, and see that she doesn't fall out of the bed."

I am dying. I must be.

"Pay no attention to the screaming, Mrs. Mick. It's the vitriol talking."

"What she saying, Doc?"

"Pa. She's says it over and over. We may have to restrain her."

Suddenly the whisker-laden face of the doctor changed into the face of a large black lion. It lunged at me. I screamed again.

Don't let him hurt me again, Pa. Why did you leave me?

"Lord, I ain't never seen so much puking, Doc, not in all my born days. Stuff's running right out her maw. Girl swallowed the Thames whole."

"I told you, the blue vitriol is drawing out the laudanum."

No, don't leave me! Not again!

"The whore's hell-bound. Why are you trying to prevent it?"

"If you want your meal and gin, you old harpy, keep silent and do as you are instructed. I won't say it again."

That is all I remember of my first night at Tothill Fields Prison.

CHAPTER IX

WHEREIN FAIRIES AND DREAMS MINGLE IN A NURSERY, AND RUBY MAKES AN UNEXPECTED FRIEND.

Georgy was downstairs going over the accounts, so I had the nursery watch. Playing with my children was a magic carpet ride to my own past. There's a power in children that is wonderful to behold. In being with them, you become one again.

Within the walls of this room, disappointing parents, rat-infested blacking factories, never-ending deadlines and other perplexities of life ceased to exist. The afternoon sun glowed through the windows and gave the parted lace curtains an ethereal shine. This was a world unto itself. It was a sanctuary.

I was seated on the floor next to Frank, who was two years old. He liked to chew toy blocks to soothe his gums, and had been rifling through one after the other like they were a box of sweets until he settled on one most suited to his palate. Apparently, the block with painted with the letter 'Q' was the most delicious of blocks.

"Blocks are for building, Frank, not eating," I said as I took a few blocks from his pile and began to build a tower. "See? You try." He copied me, and when I applauded him, he screamed in satisfaction.

Ten-year-old Charley was seated at the table looking at a book of maps. Katey sat across from him, drawing. Her face was fixed in a stern concentration.

"Papa," asked Charley, "will you ever get another bird?"

Mamie, who sat on the nursery sofa, and whose face had since been hidden by her picture book, now sprang to life in support of her brother's cause.

"Oh no!" she exclaimed, her legs swinging back and forth. "Please, Papa, Grip was so naughty."

I put another block down next to Frank, and looked up at her.

"You were very little then, Mamie," I returned.

Mamie's porcelain brow furrowed. "I wasn't any younger than Frank is now, Papa. I do remember Grip a little. He chased us and pecked our ankles." She coiled her little nose at the recollection.

"Who's Grip, Papa?" asked Walter who had now sat himself next to Frank.

"Grip died in '43, the year before you were born, Walter. He was our raven."

"What's a raven?" he asked, and put his thumb into his mouth.

"It's a great big black bird," I said as I took his thumb back out again and pointed to the drawing on the wall that Maclise had done for Catherine for our American tour back in '42. She had been loathed to leave the children behind, and the image comforted both of us during the six-month separation. Maclise had included Grip in the portrait, perching next Charley, Mamie, Katie, and Walter. "And if you don't stop sucking your thumb, your face will grow long, and you will look like a horse."

Walter giggled and whinnied around the room. Katey slammed down her pen in frustration.

"I wish *I* could fly like a bird," she said, "so I could go somewhere quiet."

"Come now, Lucifer Box," I answered as I rose and made for the table, "no sparks in the nursery."

"I am sorry, Papa," said Katey who covered her drawing as soon as I knelt down by her. "It's just that I'm nearly finished with this." I obediently averted my gaze from her paper.

"If I could fly," interjected Charley, "I would go to the top of Nelson's column. You must be able to see the whole world from up there! Where would you fly, Papa?"

The old temptation of deserting the ranks swelled in my breast again. But thoughts of Catherine's miscarriage when dear Mary had died dampened it, as was its usual custom. I did love my children. I just had more than people realized. My characters were just as real to me, just as flesh and blood as were the beings in this chamber. They were also my children. In short, the Inimitable was the father of hundreds. And all with no harem to assist me; quite the feat!

"Oh, here and there, Charley" I sighed. "Sometimes to France, sometimes to Italy..." *Sometimes never to come back here, God forgive me.*

Katey put down her pen in triumph and clapped her hands. "I would fly to the top of trees so I could watch people." Then she raised her drawing to me, "Just like my fairie. She lives in an oak tree."

"And she is very beautiful, indeed." I answered and kissed her cheek.

"Are all fairies good?" interjected Mamie, who succeeded in taking another block out of Frank's mouth. Frank responded by knocking down her block tower with a defiant "Pah!"

Then, as if sensing she would do the same to his, he destroyed his own tower, and laughed at his successful bombardment of the conversation.

"There are no such things as fairies." said Charley, who turned the page in his book.

Katey's face grimaced, and Mamie gasped.

"I beg your pardon, Flaster Floby?" I ejaculated. "I'll have you know I met one just a few days ago."

"Really, Sir?" asked Charley wearily. I was thankful he was still young enough to be swayed.

"Indeed I did, Sir."

Mamie's curls bounced on either side of her head as she bounded over to Katey and me.

"Was she pretty, Papa?" she asked.

"She was radiant, Mamie." I answered with a smile.

"What's radiant?" asked Walter.

"It means more beautiful and shining than Heaven's gates." I said.

Walter smiled. "More beautiful than Mama?" inquired my young son.

My mouth began to dry up.

"Well..."

"Oh, Papa," interrupted Katey, mercifully, "did she have wings like my drawing?"

"Of course she did, darling. They were pink, if I recall. Yes. I asked her if I might touch them and she said yes. They were as soft as a cloud."

I watched in delight as my children's eyes grew to the size dinner plates. Mamie turned to Katey.

"Katey," she said, taking the paper in her hand, "that's what your drawing is missing. This fairie is white. Only angels wear white."

"That is silly." said Charlie.

"Angels are white!" Mamie exclaimed in defense of her assumption. "Isn't that so, Papa?"

Mary's white ghost slipped into my brain and I drew Mamie to my chest and held her tightly. Mamie's impending arrival into the world had been a comfort to Catherine—a consolation from the sorrow of losing Mary. And I had named the girl after the aunt she would never know. *Oh, for the day when I am free of this body, of this life. Then I shall be able to fly…to her.*

"Papa, you're squeezing me!" Mamie exclaimed.

"Oh!" I released her and the child scurried away and smoothed her green skirts with disdain. "My darling Mild Glo'ster, I'm so sorry. But your sister is correct."

"Make the fairie blue," said Charley as he stood on his chair, drew his right hand into his sleeve, and rested his vacant cuff on his chest, "like Admiral Lord Nelson's tunic. Grandfather says that he was the greatest Englishman who ever lived!"

Katey wrinkled her nose at her brother's suggestion. "She's a fairie, Charley, not a sailor. Boys don't know anything. And I think she should be yellow."

"No, Katey," said Mamie, "it must be a more striking color. Papa, what would you choose?"

I needed no time to compose an answer.

"Lilac."

*****

Before my eyes opened, I realized the awful smell was gone. Instead of the foul muck of the Thames, I could smell straw, wool, coal smoke and liniments. My skin was swathed in dry, comfortable cotton bedclothes. I turned my head to my right. I was in a large room, long like a corridor, with plaster walls the color of smoke. Save sniffling or the occasional cough from a corner of the room, it was quiet. The room also contained windows at the far end of this chamber, and many cots made of plain wooden frames and a hearth that thankfully my own was opposite. A few of the cots were occupied by disheveled souls, some of whom looked more dead than alive. One woman, who looked about my age, was so thin her bones nearly protruded from her greenish skin. Clad in a black shawl, she sat up in bed still as a statue. I wondered whether she was already dead.

Then I felt hands on my chest and something cold pressed to it. I looked to the left and saw the face of a big, broad man leaning close over me. He was fit; his shirtsleeves were rolled up, revealing taunt, shapely forearms. They were arms full of power. His face was framed by beautifully toned cheeks, and a neat brown beard. The skin around his equally brown eyes was constricted in concentration.

Instinctively, I reached up to fend him off, but he rested my arms back to my sides with unmistakable gentleness.

"I am Dr. Wilkins. You are at Tothill Fields. You have been in and out of consciousness for a week."

"Piss off," I croaked.

Dr. Wilkins shushed me, "Let me do this, hussy. Be quiet and lay still."

"Aye," said I, "that's how they usually like it."

He laughed as he put some sort of instrument into his ears. "That's women for you. Save their life one minute, the next they're fighting to run away. Now shut up so I can listen to your heart, or I'll gag you."

His voice, low and full of tone, was not harsh. Rather than annoyed, the Doctor seemed amused by the situation, as if he had joked with my kind scores of times before. I was about to tell him what he could do with that blasted instrument when the old hag I had seen in my delirium shuffled into the room with a small tray. She was just as ugly as in my fever. Her mob cap was so dirty it looked like a web of soot perched on her head. Her once-white apron, was now as worn and foul as her body; the pocket bulged, and I could just see the cork of a bottle protruding. She was breathless as she reached my wretched bed.

"See how well you do with this broth," said Dr. Wilkins, "I'm sure Mrs. Mick will blow on it if it's too hot," he added coyly.

"The devil I will," retorted the ancient woman in a withered Irish voice. "She's awake, she can feed herself." The 's' in her words were surprisingly recognizable, considering she had no teeth.

"Well, then, don't linger on my account," I said.

I felt the bed shift as Doctor Wilkins quickly rose.

"I won't," he answered. Then he addressed the woman again. "See that she takes it all." His eyes met mine again and narrowed with a joking tone. "Or I'll hold her down and force it in."

I narrowed my own eyes back. "Ah, familiar words indeed. Kind of you to make me feel at home, Doctor."

He sucked in a quick breath of air and whistled.

"Sharp tongued, aren't you, Little Puss?" he answered, "I like that in a woman."

Over the next week he visited daily. I was moved from the large infirmary to a smaller room containing a barred window, a small fire and two beds. As if the bars were not enough, the empty bed was a reminder to me that I was lucky to be alive, but also that no one was coming for me. The young man who had pulled me from the Thames had said he would tell someone I was here. Did he mean Top, or Dandy? If he had meant Top, I was thankful that I was in a prison.

I became grateful for Wilkins's daily visits. After administering my physics, he would stay and chat. He was old enough to be my father, but certainly did not act it. His father died at sea when he was twelve, and so he was raised by his mother and grandfather. His grandfather, once a doctor himself, and had taught Joe exacting precision, discipline, and many a lewd joke. After helping to save an injured child in a Workhouse, he persuaded Joe to give up a life at sea, and secured a place for him at the London Hospital Medical College.

"You have a woman, Doc?" I asked him one day, as it was a subject we had not yet discussed.

"I've had lots of women, Puss," he answered. Puss was the pet name he had bestowed upon me, since he likened me to a drowned kitten upon arrival at the prison.

"You know what I mean," I answered.

"Aye."

"Well, then. You married?"

"Hard to keep a woman happy with the hours a doctor keeps," he grinned playfully. "How about you, Puss? Who's missing you right about now, eh?"

A foul tremor went through my body, and I looked away from him.

"No one, Boots." It was only fair that he get a pet name, too. The joke seemed to fit.

"Funny thing, if you ask me. A girl as fiery and lovely as you," he paused a moment, then added, "Pity you had to come to this to find out he didn't really love you."

I shot my head back in his direction. "How dare you. Maybe—maybe he just can't find me."

"So there is someone, then. If you ask me, he's not looking."

"Well I didn't ask you!"

"Puss," said Wilkins, "if my woman was somewhere alone and frightened, nothing would keep me from finding her."

All the muscles in my stomach tightened at his words, and I felt heat rise up in my face.

My health was his foremost care, however. Dr. Wilkins's patients had to accept his word as law. The walking was the worst part. I slowly began to realize that during some steps, I couldn't feel the ground. It was as if my feet were gone one moment, and had returned the next. Before I had been moved out of the infirmary, he had made me walk up and down the length of the room daily. I begged him to stop, but he refused.

"My legs hurt," I told him plainly.

"They're going to no matter what, Ruby. You'd be better off using them instead of spreading them. Now stop complaining like a baby and take another step."

And so it remained day after day, until one afternoon when I decided to see for myself if his torture had done its job. I edged myself off the bed and tried to stand. My arse left the bed just as he opened the door to my cell. His brown eyes flashed fright and fury all at once. He raced to my side, but was not in time to save me from collapsing to the floor.

"You damned stupid, obstinate girl!" hollered Dr. Wilkins as he hovered over me. "I told you never try to get up without someone here, or are you too stupid to remember anything? Now lay your ass back down in that bloody bed or by God I'll strap you down."

Something inside me began to burn, and I looked up at him from the floor in a rage.

"I am not stupid!" I shouted as I tried to get up and failed.

As a further sign of his indifference, Wilkins crossed his arms across his broad chest. Then he snorted, as if to confirm his amusement of my current frailty.

"You are stupid. Couldn't even drown yourself properly."

"I fell in, you bastard!" I screamed.

"A likely tale. Some little coward you are."

"Some great bloody doctor you are!" I exclaimed, and began to lash out with my arms to push him away. "Your patients must all decide to die just so they don't have to suffer you! If I'm such a bother, fuck off then, and let me lie here and join them."

With one final blow, I pounded my hands as hard as I could in his chest. Wilkins's laughter ceased, and his expression wiped clean of all humor. When he raised his arms, I thought certain he would strike me. But instead he cradled me like a ragdoll and carried me back to my bed. I struggled, embarrassed beyond belief, ordering him to let me go, but he ignored me. His hands deftly found the blankets and he covered me with an unmistakable tenderness.

"Hush. I'm sorry, Puss," His eyes shone with mirth and compassion as he smoothed down my hair. "I had to test your strength. There's more than fight left in you, my girl, there's still a fire burning down deep. Sometimes it just takes someone to help shovel a bit more coal on. But I'm afraid it means I'll have to change your prognosis."

"What?" I asked.

He chuckled softly. "You're going to live."

"Yeah?"

"Yeah."

"Right, then. From now on, it's Miss Puss to you."

From that day we achieved a somewhat complicated friendship. But there was still no questioning him when it came to his doctoring. My bedside table remained cluttered with a tumbler and numerous bottles of noxious tonics. One was the blasted blue vitriol that had caused the vomiting. Another read 'French's Sarsaparilla and Chamomile—For Purifying the Blood and Strengthening the Digestive Organs'. Bull; it tasted about as bad as the Thames. Even the water and mustard he had fed me was preferable to that. Next to the bottles lay a small box of 'King's Respiratory Lozenges'.

If this persisted, I would soon piss brown, sweat yellow, and shit blue, no doubt to his great delight.

CHAPTER X

IN WHICH MR. DICKENS AND HIS DEAR FRIEND MR. JOHN FORSTER BANTER AS ONLY FRIENDS CAN. RUBY GRANTS AN AUDIENCE WITH THE INIMITABLE.

"Charles, did you hear a word I have said?"

My pen halted and I looked up at him from my desk.

"Forster, you know I have to get this down."

"By all means, dear fellow," taunted my friend, adding a sarcastic "Don't mind me," immediately after. "*Dombey*?"

"No, the newest book on lace tatting. I needed a change. Of course it's *Dombey*!"

I did not appreciate his idiotic questions.

"Ah, Carker's interest in Mrs. Dombey is growing, I take it?" said Forster as he set the coffee down on my desk that he had just refreshed. "Brilliant, my dear Charles. The public adore it."

"They had better," I retorted, dipping my pen hard enough into the well to cause a small bit to splash out through the bottle's mouth, "especially with another little Dickens on the way." I wiped the excess ink from the pen tip. *Family is a blessing. Keep telling yourself that.* But there were times when I inwardly cursed this multiplying clan of mine. *Dombey* was my seventh novel, which made it one book per child. I was falling behind; I would surely die young if this kept up.

A knock at the door brought Georgy into the study. She handed me an envelope.

"Charles, it is from Mr. Tracey," she said.

I thanked her, read the note quickly, and felt my heart leap.

"Ruby is awake!" I shot out of my chair with delight. To blazes with Carker. My dark-haired seamstress in lilac had been found at last!

"Who?" exclaimed Georgy and Forster in unison.

"Rubina Waller," I answered, "A very interesting surname. Yes, it suits her, wouldn't you say, Forster?"

"What?" he said as I took a small piece of foolscap and scribbled a response to Mr. Tracey, informing him that I would call at eleven o'clock that morning. Georgy left to give the note to the messenger boy. By now Forster was chuckling wickedly.

"And what, pray, do you find so amusing?" I said as I reached the sofa.

He replaced his coffee cup on the table near the mantel.

"Why, Ruby, Charles," he stated, his brooding features bent into a humorous glare.

I cocked an eyebrow in response, "A new girl for Urania. She is intriguing, Forster. I think she could do very well there. We agreed to meet and discuss things. But she vanished. An informant discovered that she had been attacked. She's at Tothill Fields. The doctor there reports that she nearly died."

Forster dabbed his mouth with his napkin. "I am not surprised, Charles."

God, how that man irked me sometimes with his superior airs. But for some reason, friends tolerate the most absurd qualities in one another.

"Tracey read her my letter," I continued.

"Ah yes, your Letter To Fallen Women. Brilliant idea to have it circulated in the prisons, Charles."

"First sensible thing you've said so far, John. Tracey has excellent judgment, and I owe it to the girl to hear her out. She is…oh, Forster, she is…"

"Yeeees, Charles," said my friend, back in his usual pompous manner.

"She is…interesting," I said, rather sheepishly. *Charles, curse you for coming over like a schoolboy. You know you'll never live it down now!*

"Interesting?" he asked, his hand arcing the length of his stomach, as if to indicate an expectant woman.

I held up my palm. "Not that interesting, I hope." That was the first rule of Urania Cottage. No expectant women were allowed. Not ever. Not even one as fascinating as Ruby.

"If you say so, Charles. I wish you luck," he said as he clicked open his watch. "Well, it is half past nine now. I shall leave you to your harem."

"Correction, Forster," I retorted, "My virgin charges." A true friend (and through it all, John Forster was the truest friend any man ever had) will always appreciate the darkest of humor.

He chuckled as he made for the doorway.

"Remember, Forster," I said as I leaned down to reach for the sugar, "this is about the chance to change—"

Forster turned. "I know, my dear fellow, I know." Then with a splendidly wicked smirk across his lips, he remarked, "*And Dickens's name was good upon 'Change for anything he chose to put his hand to!*"

I brought my head down upon the table in frustration. "Confound it, Forster, the *Carol* is nearly four years old. Quote something new!"

He erupted into laughter that would have made a hyena see fit to join a silent order.

"Helluva twist, dear fellow," I retorted as I hurled a sofa cushion at him.

*****

From the moment he strode through the door, I was dumbstruck. Goddamn, it was him.

"Ruby, thank God," he whispered.

I was so taken with the sight of him I swallowed the lozenge Dr. Wilkins had given me not five minutes before. Then I struggled to find my voice.

"Dandy," was all I could utter.

Dickens laughed through his nose as he peeled off his yellow canary gloves. He removed his fine great coat of green wool with sharp velvet lapels and a brown beaver top hat. His splendor was completed by another maroon paisley waistcoat and that same thick golden watch chain, from which hung that dainty malachite pendant. Famous author he may be, but Charles Dickens was a Dandy if ever I laid eyes on one. If I had to choose his best feature, it would undoubtedly have been his eyes.

They flashed as if two tiny lamps were eternally lit inside his head.

"Mr. Dickens, I—"

He held up his hand. "No offense, my girl."

He raised a hand and brushed it through his chestnut waves. I tried to speak, but began to cough. He poured some water into the tumbler and helped me bring it to my lips. Dickens was not a large man, but his hands were strong. They encountered my weak form as if it were made of glass. I nodded my thanks and rested my head back against the headboard rails. Then I gestured to the folded paper that lay close by on the bed.

"The Governor read your letter to me. I've been looking at it some this morning on my own."

Mr. Dickens set the tumbler back down.

"Ask any thing you like. You shall have an answer."

"Where is the house?" I asked.

"Lime Grove, Shepherd's Bush," he answered. "It is known as Urania Cottage."

I shot him a wary glance, "And it ain't a prison?"

"No. There are rules there, but it is a Home. You will not be behind cold bars and devoid of care."

"What would I do there?" I began to cough again, and he handed the tumbler back to me.

"Your sewing is already impeccably sound. Use the time to improve other skills, such as housekeeping. You will have your own small garden to tend in the warmer months."

"Teacups and roses don't suit me, Mr. Dickens," I said, eying him over the brim of the tumbler as I took another sip, "Respectable people aren't going to give me custom in this city. Not for clothes, anyway."

He moved to the chair near my bed and crossed his legs. Strike me dead, I had never seen green check trousers that loud in my life. On any other man they would have looked ghastly, clownish. But on Mr. Dickens, they were striking and smart, like him. I took one more sip as he began to speak again.

"But it is more than that, Ruby. Think of the example you could set for the other girls there. You have much to offer, I believe."

My only reply was a shrug of my shoulders. "What do I get?"

"After a year or so of instruction," he continued, "passage will be purchased for you on a ship bound for Australia. There you will be assisted in finding a good and stable situation. You may even find a husb—"

Dickens ducked to his left and narrowly escaped a small shower of horizontal rain.

"Are you mad?" I exclaimed in between choked intakes of breath. "Australia?"

He took out his handkerchief and handed it to me. "Why not? No one knows you there."

"No one knows me in Scotland, neither, so couldn't I go there instead of halfway around the bleeding world? And what's all this about a husband? You running a bloody harem or something? I don't want to be married."

His eyes narrowed slightly. "The more I know, the more I can help you. No one at the Home will know anything about you. Speaking of one's past is forbidden there. But will you tell me, please, about your parents? Let us begin with your father."

I shot him a look fit to melt stone. "He never hurt me."

"I am very glad to hear it. I understand that he taught you to sew."

"Aye, and very well, too."

"And what of your mother?" asked Dickens.

"She couldn't help herself. That's all I'll say."

His gaze became hard, and he began to twist the small ring on his finger.

"It was her fault," he muttered as if he were conversing with himself. Was it my imagination, or was he was shivering slightly? If he was, it passed seconds later, and he continued as if nothing had happened. Then his gaze found mine again, and a knowing overtook his features.

"Who can I help you escape from?" he asked.

"I'm tired. I'd like to sleep now."

"Ruby, please trust me."

I still would not look at him.

"You might as well go," I said quietly, "I've no wish to be married and it's obvious that is what you intend for me. Men always want something in return, and they don't give a damn how they get it. You say I need a man to take care of me. Well I say it's better to be a hired hand than an unpaid slave. Either hell is still a hell."

Dickens sighed.

"Ruby, with a fresh countenance, I am sure any decent fellow would be glad to lay eyes upon you and cherish you as his Lady."

"You don't know a goddamned thing. Get out." Dickens leaned closer.

"Is burying the past worth burying yourself?"

I turned and struck him. In my weakened state, it was not a blow of any consequence. He drew back, but his eyes never left me.

"You dare to judge me!" I shouted with heavy breath, "When were you ever abandoned by your mother and father and left to fend for yourself! I wish I had died and I ain't sorry. Bloody Dandy Toff, I'll be damned if you're going to make a doll out of me. Or a virgin, for that matter. You don't know a goddamned thing!"

The tears arrived then, along with Doctor Wilkins. I lay there a blubbering fool. Dickens ordered him away.

"It's only because of the fever, I know," he said to the doctor. "It is nothing."

"Mr. Dickens, her fever has not completely left her," said Wilkins as sternly as he had addressed me during my first days at the prison. "Do not over excite her, Sir, or I will insist that you leave. Is that understood?"

Dickens waved his hand with an air of dismissal. "Yes yes, I understand. Now please leave us."

Wilkins looked down at me. "Holler if you need me."

I smiled at him, "I will." He took his leave, but I knew he wouldn't go far. Dickens placed his hand tentatively on my shoulder. He did not speak right away. I found it strange that a man who was famous for writing words could not summon anything to say to a harlot. When he did finally speak, his voice was a gentle whisper.

"Please tell me." He said it the way my father had when nightmares broke my sleep. Father had said then that nightmares were not real. How wrong he had been.

Dickens took my hand in his and patted it. I tried to remove my hand from his, but he kept his grip. So I threw the tumbler blindly like an unwanted toy. It crashed onto the floor. With my free hand, I tried to pull the blankets over my head, and wait for death.

"You're not going to escape that easily," said Mr. Dickens, his voice now raised. "One good turn deserves another. You began the wager, but I shall emerge the victor."

His grip on my hand increased as I tried to pry it free. His gaze was intense. I grit my teeth and glared at him.

"Let go of me," I ordered hoarsely.

"You tempted me, Ruby," said Dickens, "and you failed. One good turn deserves another. My offer is even more delicious than yours, and your outburst proves me right."

Now I began to struggle in earnest. He was frightening me.

"What does it prove?" I asked.

It was now his turn to lean close to my face.

"That you want it back."

His voice was now dry and husky, and his eyes searched mine, as if he believed he could hypnotize me. Perhaps he was, because I suddenly realized I had stopped struggling. And he knew it; he began to brush my eyebrows with his thumbs.

"Want— want what back?"

"Your innocence. Time can be erased, Ruby. Innocence can be regained. I can give that to you."

"Impossible," I whispered. That fire in his eyes! Didn't Dickens mean devil? Oh Christ, was he really mad after all?

He sensed my fear, and sat back in the chair running a hand through his long hair. Absentmindedly, his hands found each other, and he began to twist the ring on his little finger again.

"You are beautiful, Ruby. You have intelligence and talent. Yes, you may be small, but your will is as fierce as the stones of this building. Once I knew a girl, much like you in several ways, though never on the streets. She died. Young."

"Mary?" I asked.

He looked at me in fear.

"How did you know that?"

"You said her name that night in my room."

He swallowed hard. "Yes, that was her name. Perfection she was. And I see so many women on the street, who deserve the long life that girl was denied, and they are convinced they do not deserve it!"

Charles Dickens seemed on the verge of tears, and began pacing the room in an attempt to quell them.

"Why do you value yourself so little?" he snapped as he continued to pace.

"Because I'm a whore," I answered plainly, thinking his question ridiculous.

"Then the logical course of action would be to no longer *be* one!" he shouted. "I am handing that chance to you, so reach out your hand and take it!"

"Mr. Dickens," I said, hoping to calm him down, "I mean no offense. But even if I were to change, how could I hope to be accepted by—?"

"That is why you will go to Australia," he interrupted, gesturing behind him as if Australia were somewhere on the other side of the wall. "It's as new and as far removed from London as a human being can get!"

"But I don't want to go there." *Not the wisest thing to say at this juncture, Ruby!*

"How do you know?" Dickens shouted, fit to explode. "You have never been there!"

"Have you?" I retorted.

Then Dickens stopped pacing.

"That is not the point," he retorted, placing a hand on his thin hip.

I knew I had him.

"You've never been there either, have you?" I said, crossing my arms across my chest.

The great writer licked his lips and pursed them tightly. His face was fast approaching the color of his waistcoat.

"Ruby, you are trying my pat—"

"Don't you get high and mighty with me, you pompous twit! Out there in the world people may kiss your ass for pulling faerie tales out of it, but I'll be damned if I ever will. Now you've never been to this god-forsaken colony, and yet you expect me to go there? Kindly inform me just what in hell is so bloody marvelous about

Australia? If you're in love with it so much, why don't you go there and stop bothering me!"

He stood there, motionless, mouth agape, as if he had never been spoken to like that in his life. I didn't know what he would do next, nor did I care. This was the second time I had rendered this famous man completely speechless, and I was finding it not only enjoyable, but highly addictive.

"It is a new colony where the prospects are so numerous the scales cannot hold them. It is perfect." His tone was much subdued now.

"Perfect?" I interrupted. "You mean perfect for men to find a bride. I told you I don't want—"

He hopped back into his chair.

"Well, perhaps you will feel differently later on." He said it sweetly, like a little boy hoping to make up with his cross mother. Lord of mercy, this man's emotions bounced quicker than a ball! "Besides, would you rather remain here?"

"I don't know," I answered, my eyes brimming.

Dickens stood, and reached for his top hat and took out his gloves.

"My offer is unchanged," he said as he put on his gloves. "There is a place at Urania Cottage for you whenever you want it."

And then he walked out.

CHAPTER XI

WHEREIN OUR MR. DICKENS PETITIONS THE WEALTHY MISS COUTTS, AND RUBY EXPERIENCES MORE OF TOTHILL FIELD'S PRISON.

Before leaving the prison I had arranged with Tracey that Ruby should stay there until she was well. By then she would say yes to the Home. I would see to that. And in the meantime there would be plenty to occupy her; there was a clothing shop within the prison. As her health improved she could pass the time there. It only remained to notify Miss Burdett Coutts of my new find and persuade her to grant Ruby entry into Urania.

The chilled air assaulted me as I walked along, like a balm to my blood. Dear God, the anger in that girl's eyes at the betrayal of her mother; the horror she had been abandoned to. It cut me as swiftly as a sword.

"When were you ever given up by your mother?"

My cheek did not sting where she had struck me. Rather, it was my soul that burned. The betrayal of a mother is an unforgivable offense. I should know. I *did* know. It invades my waking dreams still. No. 30 Strand is an address I avoid with a passion. For a moment I had entertained the notion of telling Ruby about my time there. What was more, I had begun to tell her about Mary. What was wrong with me? I wanted to tell her, but I could not tell her. I could tell no one. Dear God in Heaven, I could not!

Could Ruby reform and succeed? I would give her the chance at the very least. Damn, she was sharp. Her reaction to Australia was also the standard; most of the girls recoiled at the mention of it.

As with many of the others with whom I had conversed, Ruby's past seemed just under the surface, about to boil over like a pot of potatoes left too long on the hob. Could a new chance help her to move that pot off the hob before the lid shot off? Those thoughts hammered in my brain as I arrived at Miss Coutts's home in time for tea. With her approval, Ruby's fate could be changed forever.

"There is something about her—"

"Yes, yes," said Miss Coutts as she added cream to my cup, "full of goodness. So Mr. Brownlow said about young Oliver Twist. But this is reality, Charles. Give me a reason."

"Miss Coutts, her dress was no rag," I answered.

"Full of goodness and thievery, I perceive, then."

"They may not have been a Lady's finery to match yours," I said, gesturing to my interrogator, clad in finest purple silk, "but she possesses a degree of skill with a needle. Her father was a tailor; now that further suggests that she is far above amateur in her skills. Ruby Waller is not without talent or morals. She should be considered. Nay, she should be admitted."

Urania's Benefactress handed me my cup and poured her own.

"I am not so certain, Charles. From your account it would appear that darker forces are at work within this girl."

I paused just as the cup touched my lips, and set it back on the saucer.

"State your meaning, if you please, Madam."

She coolly swallowed a sip of tea.

"My meaning is simple," answered Miss Coutts, "You know her present, yet you know nothing of her history."

My collar began to grow warm. "And what, pray, does that matter?" I asked, "She will tell us in time."

The brow of her long thin face creased. Her skin was sprinkled with patches of red, rough skin. Her mother remarked once that it was from taking too much coffee.

"Charles," she answered, "we need to know if Ruby can be trusted."

I could not believe my ears. At length it was the sound of my saucer colliding with the table which broke the silence as I bolted out of my chair.

"You think of this now? Or have your other engagements with the Duke of Wellington once again made you forget what this house is meant to do? Do we honestly know that any of them can be trusted? No. But nothing will be gained if we do not try, Miss Coutts. Bad faith on our parts will only breed distrust among them, and that would be a death blow to the whole thing!"

Her eyes narrowed above her pink, spotted cheeks. Her voice was quiet, but every word punctured the hull of my temper.

"Sit down this minute."

Damn. If I lose her money, it's all up!

Slowly, I reclaimed my seat.

"You may have conceived of this venture, Charles," said Miss Coutts as cool as if she were addressing a rosebush, "but kindly remember who is funding it. May I remind you that you did not deem me fit to see this place until it was up to your standards? It seems that in the end you need no one's opinion but your own."

"I am sorry, Miss Coutts," I said as quickly as I could yet make it sound genuine. "But if I felt this girl to be lost already, I would not be so insistent."

She dabbed the corner of her mouth with her napkin of a pale linen.

"And when are you ever not insistent?"

I made to answer, but she held up her hand. Her pursed lips formed into a small smile.

"Miss Waller shall go to Urania as soon as she is well enough. But do not forget yourself again, Charles."

"Thank you Miss Coutts. I shall not," said I as I reached for my teacup and saucer, "But this Home will do some good," I raised my teacup as if to offer a toast to our agreement, "I know the idea is a good one."

"And how do you know that, pray?"

I smiled at her, "Because it is mine."

*****

It was about a week after I had seen Dandy when they started me in the sewing room. Row upon row of girls, seated on hard benches, all with identical dark dresses, white pinners and house caps, sewing in silence all day long. We were being kept to our place; no one to chat with, nothing but work and repentance. You would have found more life in an undertaker's shop at half past midnight than in that sewing room at half past noon.

Then I woke one morning with a searing pain in my left leg. It was as if cotton and wool had been substituted in the dead of night for iron and rock, and I struggled to free my leg from the covers and sheets. I heard the door open and saw a flicker of light coming closer. It was Mrs. Mick. Her lips were curled back, and the candle light reflected off her black, dead gums. I couldn't tell if the expression on her face was a smile or repulsion, but regardless she made no move to help me. I barked at the hag to fetch Dr. Wilkins. When he eventually arrived, he lit the lamp, and I could finally see my leg. Resting on the white sheet, my left big toe and its surrounding flesh resembled a plated cold ham in both color and proportion. Wilkins told me I had the gout.

"No doubt resulting from an overabundance of gin and laudanum," said he, "It can be gotten rid of, but it will take time."

Grotesque as it was and despite the ungodly concoctions Wilkins would no doubt inflict upon me, the gout saved me from having to go back to that damned sewing room. Therefore I embraced my affliction with the relish of a Saint.

And so the daily regimen of Lithia water and wrapping my foot in cloth strips soaked in belladonna began. My limbs ached to move from the bed I had occupied for what seemed like centuries. I missed the sunlight. When Mr. Tracey came to me and said, "You will work from your bed", I had to cover my face with my hands to conceal the smile. Isn't that what had ended me up in here?

My thoughts went back to Top. Where was he? Was he trying to find me?

Damn it to hell! I would go to this crazy Cottage of Dandy's, toe the line (as sailors are fond of saying), and then run away at the dockside or jump ship en route to Australia. I could always find some man who would befriend a girl like me. All my thoughts turned to it, and with each stitch I sewed, the pattern of my plan began to take form.

And then, one afternoon, I heard a knock at the door. Mr. Dickens entered. His clothing was as loud as I remembered, though this time of a blue and yellow theme. Under his left arm he carried a brown paper parcel, which he proudly handed to me. Inside, there lay a cotton dress with white and blue waves that swam from collar to hem.

"I thought you could do with a change, as the garments here are abhorrently boring," he said. I took this as the closest to an apology that I was going to receive, but I didn't care. I loved dresses. Top spoiled me with them, but I always altered them to my own tastes. But now that mad, foppish bastard was useless to me. Far be it from me to turn down finery from another man who offers it.

"You couldn't have been more right, Sir," I said to Dickens.

He cocked an auburn eyebrow.

"Sir, is it? Tut, Ruby. Surely they have not taught you manners?"

I shrugged indifferently.

"Fine then. Push off, you good for nothing sod."

"That's better!" he roared. "But mind yourself at the Home," he added with a wink.

Dickens stayed much longer this time, and conducted himself as if we were lifelong friends, as if the upstart of our previous interview had never occurred. I, on the other hand, was not so ready to forget about it. But he had made an impressive gesture, and I did appreciate it.

Mrs. Mick shuffled in with a tea tray, probably at the insistence of Mr. Tracey. How her bent, wasted form made it to the bedside table was an act of God. She puffed like a dying train all the way back out the door. After she had left, Dickens rose and did the most wonderful impression of her. It was perfect, down to the humped back and the drool. Just days before, I had never wanted to see this man again. Now I was clapping like a little girl seeing her first Punch and Judy performance. Lord, this man was good at getting his own way.

Dickens gave a grand bow, like an actor upon the stage. Then he resumed his seat and took a small note book from his breast pocket, along with a small pencil. I had never met anyone so inquisitive, and behind that politeness I knew where his curiosity was really rooted. My past. But at this meeting he thankfully did not press the matter.

He was very interested to know how I was faring and anything else I "would care to divulge". He nodded and took notes as I told him of my gout, Mrs. Mick and Doctor Wilkins. Then he told me of Miss Coutts (the rich lady who paid for the Home and my dress), and of Mrs. Holdsworth, the Matron, who would collect me on the day appointed.

"She can be difficult and is entirely uninteresting," he said dismissively. "But the home is run well."

"So you still think I'm coming, then?" I interjected.

"I know you are. Besides, if you don't I shall take back the dress."

I smiled coyly at him.

"Dandy, I'd like to see you try."

When Doctor Wilkins came in and told Dickens in so many words that I needed my rest, he took my hand in both of his before leaving his chair.

"Mrs. Holdsworth will come in a fortnight for you. I will see you at the Home."

"Maybe," I winked.

Dickens smiled all the same, and strode out. He knew he'd won.

The morning before I was to leave Tothill Fields, Mr. Tracey came and took coffee with me. He complimented me on my sewing, and told me I could take one thing I had made with me. I asked for the bonnet I had repaired three days ago, since I did not have one of my own. He told me I could have it, and wished me well.

Doctor Wilkins paid me one last visit after Mr. Tracey left. He quickly examined me and seemed satisfied with my improvement, but was strangely quiet. His hand trembled when he reached into his bag. He set a small brown papered parcel on my bed, and stood up.

"I don't know that you'll like them," he said quickly, "but I know you don't have any."

I pulled the paper apart to reveal a pair of grey leather gloves. They were a perfect fit.

"If you ever need a Friend, please come to me without fear. Remember my address?"

"Yes. Burton Crescent. I remember. Thank you." It didn't seem enough of a response for such a kind gesture, but I truly couldn't think of anything else to say to him.

"Joe," he said gently.

"Thank you. Joe."

Wilkins raised my hand and bought it to his lips. They touched with all the harshness of a flower petal. My heart quickened. But then he released my hand and made his way quickly to the door. He did not look at me, but turned his head in my direction, and whispered softly over his shoulder to me as he left.

"Good luck, Ruby."

The muscles in my stomach tightened all at once. Somewhere deep inside me, a voice urged me to shout for him. But I did not heed it. All during that last afternoon, my hands shook as I tried to thread the eye of my needle. It would take several attempts each time before the thread found its path. By three o'clock I had temporarily lost the ability to discern a French knot from a backstitch, at which point I ceased work on the clothes and slept until supper.

Throughout that long night, in the stifling silence, anticipation and dread were my constant companions. Why was I so nervous? What was there left to be afraid of that I hadn't experienced already?

The cascade of the next morning's sunlight made me momentarily blind as I stepped out of the women's entrance of Tothill Fields. It was hours before morning exercise, so there was no one about as we approached into the yard this November morning. As we neared the door, I beheld the enormous black lion's head knocker, which clutched a ring in its teeth thicker than a man's thumb. I had thought it was only from the nightmarish fever I had endured that this image even existed. But now realizing I had been carried in to the prison this way, I shuddered. The foreboding iron sentinel regarded me as I walked past. *This will be the last time you see me, you lion's head of death!*

I was clad in the dress Dandy had given me, the pair of gloves from Dr. Wilkins, the simple bonnet I had been allowed to make, and a thick shawl. My gouty foot felt much better, and I could walk relatively easily. But I held onto Doctor Wilkins's arm as a precaution. At least, that is what I kept telling myself.

Outside, I could see a waiting hansom cab, the horse exhaling thick, deep clouds that sought their way home skyward. Beside the cab stood a woman in a black and green dress with a cloak of matching colors. Her features were not quite the pointed, pinched she-dragon I had expected, but nonetheless her countenance suggested a lifetime of living by prudence and common sense. Mr. Tracey presented her to me as Mrs. Holdsworth. I curtsied to my new matron as best I could, and she returned me a curt nod. Before leaving I insisted on shaking Mr. Tracey's hand, and added a curtsey to him for Mrs. Holdsworth's benefit.

I noticed Mrs. Mick lingering just inside the door of the prison, her eyes set as stony as they ever were. But today there was an added glint of pondering, as if she could not remember what the world looked like beyond the gates. Then her reality struck me; she would never leave this place. What she had done to end up here I did not know. But, ancient witch that she was, Mrs. Mick had done me right. So I kissed the wrinkled jut of bone that was her cheek, knowing that such a public act of affection would gall her. She turned, unmoved, and disappeared back into the prison.

Dr. Wilkins helped me into the cab. I held on to his hand a bit longer than proper, and had to let my eyes convey my gratitude, since my throat was tight with emotion. He smiled gently back at me. But this smile held no trace of the joking, mischievous bear of a man I had first hated and then come to admire. The smile did not linger, and his face soon sank into sadness. He gently slipped his hand from mine, picked up the fur rug from the seat and put it around me. Then he quickly left my side without saying a word. I turned my head away and bit my lip, ashamed that I was so moved by what was nothing more than professional compassion.

The driver's whip came down from above like an oversized fishing pole, and the horse obeyed. As the cab turned and exited the gates of Tothill Fields,

I had never felt been so sad, so happy and so frightened in all my life.

CHAPTER XII

MISS RUBINA WALLER ARRIVES AT URANIA COTTAGE.

I was grateful for the distraction of the view of the market sellers setting up their stands, the colors of their fresh food swimming in a sea of early shoppers and shouting peddlers, each beginning a new day. Men and women, laden with everything from cod to clothes, all mixed with the smell of bread. My mouth, having of late only known gruel and medicines, flushed moist.

Once before I had been picked up in a hansom and taken to a new home. Now I was in a hansom again, going to another house. What lay ahead of me now couldn't possibly be worse than what I had known, but I still didn't understand how in hell was it going to be better. This time instead of fear it was my foot which prevented the option of jumping, but somewhere deep inside me, I still wanted to. I turned to Mrs. Holdsworth, who still had not spoken to me.

"Is it far, Ma'am?"

"It is."

One of the wheels passed quickly over something on the cobbles. It sent a searing bolt of heat through my leg, and I bit my lip to disguise my cursing. The sight of Mrs. Holdsworth closing her eyes in frustration told me she had understood exactly what I said.

"Beg pardon, Ma'am. It's the gout," I explained. "Strange, ain't it? I thought only fat old men suffered from it!"

"I have been informed of your complaint by Mr. Dickens," said Mrs. Holdsworth, ignoring my joke. "I dare say there is not anything about his girls he does not know."

There was a grain of condescension in her voice that made me completely forget the pain in my leg.

"Strong words for your employer," I rebutted as I adjusted my gloves.

Her tawny eyes rolled a full circle as she sucked her teeth. Then her right hand clutched the keys that hung from her chatelaine, but I don't think she was conscious of it.

"My employer, indeed. Miss Angela Burdett Coutts is my employer. It is her house, as much as he, in his greatness and genius, may like to think otherwise."

I agreed that the man was stubborn, but this woman's arrogance seemed to damn near match his. But Mr. Dickens did not need me to defend him, and I owed it him to not start things on a bad foot. And mine was bad enough already.

"Ah, well, yes. Well, I hope I shall prove of benefit, Ma'am."

As soon as she heard my words, her hand moved away from her keys.

"So do we all, child." Then she turned and looked at me. Her face was devoid of whatever anger she had felt within the past few moments.

"You must not think that I am not eager to help you, Ruby. I own that I am out of sorts. Mr.

Dickens knows that I detest getting up early, and therefore arranged for me to meet you at this ungodly hour. He likes to have his way. I have the utmost sympathy and admiration for Mrs. Dickens. He would try the patience of the Virgin Mary."

The hansom turned left again. There were many fields visible now that we were out of the city. I felt the desperate need to change the subject, and did so quickly.

"Mrs. Holdsworth, how many girls are there in the cottage?"

"You shall make four, my dear."

When Urania Cottage finally came into view, I was shocked by how small it was. I wasn't expecting a palace, but nestled in amongst other cottages and fields, there didn't seem to be enough room for all of us in there. Mrs. Holdsworth seemed to sense my question and answered it.

"There is ample room. Houses can sometimes be deceiving on the outside."

I nodded in assent. She was more right than she knew.

My new matron helped me out of the hansom and paid the driver. The man was young and had lovely greenish eyes that sparkled when he saw me smile at him. For a moment, they reminded me of Top's. The man returned the smile and tipped his cap.

"Best of luck, Little Miss," said the driver.

"Thank you," I returned.

Mrs. Holdsworth conveyed her displeasure at my fraternizing by pulling my arm a bit harder than necessary, and the driver hastened down the road.

The short path to the door was framed in a round arch (one of the books I later read said that the proper term was 'Roman'). The house looked to be of two floors, not very old, and with nothing grand about it. Mrs. Holdsworth reached to her waist for one of the keys on her chatelaine. Once we were inside, I removed my gloves and was shown where to hang my bonnet and shawl. I was ushered through a small foyer, through a door on the left, and invited to sit on a lovely green plush velvet chair, all without seeing another living soul.

"Your first task is to listen to the following instructions. They come from Mr. Dickens personally, and are read to every girl upon her arrival..."

The letter was, in a word, concise. Nothing was left out. It told me what I could say, what I could do, when I could do it, and what would happen if I didn't.

"Here we..."

Thou shalt...

"...rise at six o'clock..."

No rest for the wicked.

"Prayers at a quarter to eight. Then breakfast..."

Is the food a reward for lying?

"At half past ten, you will attend school in the parlour for two hours..."

Thank you Father for teaching me to read and cipher. Oh hell, please don't make me learn French!

"Dinner is at one o'clock, then an hour for recreation..."

Recreation? I shudder to think.

"Evening prayers are at half past eight…"

Shit. Doesn't God have anything else to do by that time of night?

"We go to sleep at nine o'clock…"

And do we get a lullaby if we're good little girls?

"And you will attend Church every Sunday. You will also be given marks for cleanliness and telling the truth…"

Dandy, I am going to strangle the bloody life out of you.

The large fire in the room was making me drowsy, but I did my best to feign interest at Mrs. Holdsworth's recitation of the Cottage Commandments. Finally, she asked me if I understood what she had read, and I told her I had. She rose, opened the door, and called out into the foyer.

"Mrs. Fisher?"

A small, younger woman in a blue fan front dress and white pinner scurried in. The lace-trimmed housecap on her head bounced along with the yellow sausage curls that hung over her ears, and she smiled pleasantly at me. Despite the sprinkling of freckles, her face was very pretty. But her chin jutted forward at an angle that, combined with her long broad nose, reminded me of the features of a cat.

Ha! Had I spoken my mind in that moment, I would have been thrown out for certain. Be the hell with it. To me, from now until doomsday, this woman would be known as Kitty Fisher! Being nicknamed after the most infamous of London whores – now there's a thing worthy of Urania

Cottage! Hell, that alone entitled her to be running the damn place.

"Ruby," said the Matron, "this is Mrs. Fisher. She assists me in the running of the home. You will obey her as you would me."

"Welcome to Urania Cottage, Ruby," said the little kitty as she extended her hand warmly.

I knew that if I moved my leg to curtsey, not only would it hurt, but I would also wet the carpet from my constrained laughter. So I took her hand and smiled instead. She slipped her arm in mine with the fondness of a woman about to promenade the park with her dearest friend and led me across the hall to another door.

Her manner was completely different from Mrs. Holdsworth in every way, and I made a point to remember to thank Mr. Dickens for selecting her. I could see that her sleeves were not correctly adjusted to her size. The right shoulder looked particularly worn. The fabric was studded by what appeared to be tiny pin pricks. I thought I might not have much faith in her if she could not even set a sleeve properly. Sleeves are like life, they are difficult to get right the first time.

The room revealed itself to be the parlour, with a large window on the front wall, framed by green velvet curtains. Three girls sat busy at their tasks around a large round table, covered with a velvet tablecloth of a striking scarlet. An open sewing basket sat on top of it, with pins, a rainbow of thread, and bone crochet hooks visible inside. A pair of large silver scissors sat on a half open bolt of the most delicious blue silk fabric I had ever seen.

One girl had a cut of that fabric in her hands, and was sewing what looked to me to be a waistband for a new skirt. Another girl was attempting to gather (though not very well) the pleats of a house cap, while the last was reading. They each looked up at me, and rose to their feet. Their dresses were as far from the common street garb as I would have imagined. And with stripes, dots, flowers and ribbons, they were as bright as any girl, especially ones like us, could have wished. But one look in their eyes told me who they really were.

"Girls, allow me to present Miss Rubina Waller. She has come to join you. Give courtesy to her."

The girls curtsied and murmured a collective jumble of words that, between them, constituted a welcome. I wished them a good morning and returned the curtsey as best I could. If I live to be a thousand years old, I will never comprehend that ridiculous ritual. The idiot fellow who invented it may have thought it genteel, but to me it looked like a hen who discovers to her horror that her egg has been replaced with a hot coal.

Then I realized the girls were staring at me. Let them. All I wanted was to plunge my hands into that sewing basket. Mrs. Holdsworth took her leave, saying that she would speak to me later. No sooner had the door closed behind her than the black haired young woman in the yellow flowered print dress stepped out from the table.

"I'm Julia. Sit here, if you like, Rubina."

Mrs. Fisher began walking me to the chair, but I was growing tired of being ushered like an old cripple. I wanted no favoritism, and gently removed my arm from Mrs. Fisher's.

"Thank you, Mrs. Fisher, but I am quite capable. And I'd be obliged if you all were to call me Ruby," I said, hoping it was polite enough.

"Ruby it is. And these are Rosina and Mary Anne." Julia gestured to each.

We sat for a few moments, simply regarding each other. Blue eyes met brown, blonde hair beheld chestnut and black. Unspoken questions perfumed the room. What have you done to be here? Were your sins worse than mine? Can I trust you? Cross me and you'll regret it! A parlour of whores and thieves clad in frocks the colors of youth, delight, and purity. We looked like ladies, yet the truth was never far away. What a lark it all seemed.

I was within an arm's length of the sewing basket now, and I could see the array of silk, satin, and grosgrain ribbons stored neatly inside. But it was that bolt of blue silk fabric that I was interested in. Mary Anne, clad in a mold-green dress with black band trim, was sitting closest to it. The color of the dress was all wrong for her mouse-colored hair, which was braided crudely and pinned in a setting at the base of her head. She had dull blue eyes, the left of which was flecked with yellow in the bottom left corner. Her frame was that of a girl of twelve, but her hands were those of a man—her fingers were thick and coarse.

"May I see that bolt of blue silk?" I asked her.

"You can see it fine from where you are," she answered.

Trust was not something any of us were used to. Mrs. Fisher gave her an encouraging look, but it made no impact.

"I'm not likely to run away with it, now am I?" I said, hoping to prove my sincerity.

"Mary Anne," said Kitty, "remember the rules."

"I am," answered Mary Anne, not taking her eyes off of me, "but Ruby did not say please."

The other girls dared not move. Had we been anywhere else, my first inclination would have been to break Mary Anne's nose. The metal of the newest hen in the coop was being tested. But this slight, bit of a girl was not so sly if she thought one snooty remark was enough to ruffle my feathers. This bitch was not going to get me, let alone on my first day. I would play her foolish game, for now. I rolled my face into a smile as I had done a thousand times for men, and sang out a calm response.

"Very well" I said demurely. "Please?"

"Please what?" she said with arrogance that only the young can possess.

"Please would you pass me that bolt of fabric?" *So I can bludgeon your goddamned face with it?*

Mary Anne took the bolt and tossed it toward me. It landed on the table with a thud, and Rosina yelped in surprise.

"Thank you," I said coolly.

It was the most sensuous thing I had ever touched. My fingers became drunk with its smoothness. If my illness did kill me, I wanted no dress. I wanted only to be wrapped in silk, like a fly in a spider web, and shrivel in eternal submission. A silk dress was about the only thing Mr. Dickens would get me to marry. Why then did I suddenly wonder what Joe would think of the material?

"Mary Anne, you idiot!" exclaimed Julia. "Now you've woken him for certain."

"What do I care?" answered Mary Anne, who folded her arms and leaned back in her chair.

"Him?" I asked.

"Yes, Ruby hasn't met him yet," Rosina answered in an excited, rapid voice, "Can he please come out now, Mrs. Fisher?"

"Can't you think about anything else?" said Julia.

"No," answered Rosina, who sat back in her chair and giggled. "I like him."

"So do I," returned Julia. "I haven't kissed him since yesterday afternoon. He may not be the best, but he's all we've got."

"As if you've ever had better, Julia," exclaimed Rosina, "I think him a very handsome fellow."

"What do any of you lot know about men, anyhow?" interjected Mary Anne.

My heart began to beat intensely as I glanced under the sofa. No one there. I stretched out my good leg under the table. No unusual shapes ensconced within reach of my toes. There were no cupboards that I could see in the room, so that option was also ruled out. Where in hell did they hide the bloke, up the fucking chimney? And the assistant matron in on it, too? From the glow in their eyes, he must have been damned good. I doubted this was what Mr. Dickens meant in the rules when Mrs. Holdsworth mentioned daily recreation! Kitty's devilish grin only increased my anxiety.

"I was wondering how long you lot could hold out before you wanted him again," she said, "Very well. After all, the poor dear has been locked up since last night. Rosie, fetch some of the bread crusts leftover from breakfast. But be quiet. We don't want Mrs. Holdsworth to hear."

Rosina obeyed. Kitty walked to the far left side of the window, and the other girls, save Mary Anne, followed close behind. They couldn't have flown out of their seats more quickly if their skirts had been on fire. What kind of a house was this?

In the corner, I saw a large shape covered in a black cloth that I hadn't noticed before. The girls took turns cooing softly and whistling as Kitty removed the cloth. It was a cage. Inside it, a small yellow and green canary was sitting still. When the light from the window hit his face, the bird chirped and began to strut all around. He seemed just as anxious to see the girls as they were to see him. Little did he know that not too long ago some of us were cooing at another type of fellow. I laughed with relief and thought it funny how a simple bird could charm some of the most hardened of street girls. Animals are much like whores, they'll never let on if they don't mind your company as long as you feed them.

Kitty opened the cage, and the bird walked up her arm until it reached her shoulder. I now understood the reason for the sleeve alterations. The bird gazed all around the room with its small, dark eyes.

"Ruby," she said, "this is Rex, the only male lodger at Urania Cottage."

"Oh!" I said. "That's him, then?"

Julia giggled. "Why Ruby, whatever did you think we meant?"

Then we all, save Mary Anne, burst into half-stifled laughter as Kitty walked over back to the table and took the seat next to me. The bird was very handsome, and his eyes had a questioning in them that I found pleasant and intriguing. Mrs. Fisher grinned at me.

"Hold your hand up to my shoulder, dear."

I had never held a bird before, but I did as she said. Rex gripped my fingers with his twig-like feet. He didn't weigh any more than a length of ribbon, and he was as soft as a beaver pelt. He looked at me the way that young cab driver had, with honest eyes.

In that moment I understood why the girls adored him. This creature did not judge them. He was perhaps the only man they had ever trusted. Past sins meant nothing to Rex, for what do birds know of conscience and regret? I held Rex up to my lips, and kissed his downy head. He chirped in acknowledgement of my supposition.

"I think Rex has made another conquest!" exclaimed Rosina, who now had returned with a saucer of crumbled bread crusts. We took turns feeding him crumbs.

Later I was given a tour of the rest of the rooms, save the upstairs, which was mercifully reserved for later that evening. As it was a Sunday, we had no schooling, and spent the better part of the afternoon in reading and having a discussion of the Beatitudes. Being new, I was mercifully allowed to listen and not obliged to comment much. *Blessed are the poor, my arse...*

The kitchen was large but not overly so, with white-washed walls and a great sink of granite at the back window. Bushels of onions, potatoes, carrots, and other vegetables, along with crocks of flour and sugar were all neatly positioned about the room. The sight of it all made me pause, and I had to swallow to rid my mouth of the flood of hunger that had possessed it. A nicer kitchen I had never seen. I was put to work in a chair at the table, slicing the freshly baked bread to accompany the Winter Vegetable Soup that was being prepared for our dinner, or so it said on the open page of our cookery book, *The American Frugal Housewife*. After our meal, I was sat back at the kitchen table drying dishes when the clock struck half noon. Not long after, the door opened.

"Come, Ruby," said Mrs. Holdsworth, "Miss Coutts and Mr. Dickens are here to see you."

Julia smiled. I passed Mary Anne in the hall, who was sweeping the floor boards just in front of the parlour door. The dust she had brewed with the broom made me cough. When I did, I heard a soft click of her tongue just as she walked by me. I ignored it and smoothed my skirts as Mrs. Holdsworth opened the door.

"Go on in, girl," she said. "And for heaven's sake, make a good impression."

Dickens, dressed in his usual bright garments, was standing at Rex's cage. They were having a grand chat from what I could tell. A woman, dressed in finery, was seated at the parlour table.

She wore a blue-grey silk dress with four flounces on the skirt, lace cuffs of a fresh cream, gold earrings and bracelet with garnets. Her lace-trimmed bonnet matched her gown. The thin, angular face it framed was as delicate as the rest of her. Such a lady I had never seen.

"Good afternoon." I said, not knowing what else to do.

Dandy turned when he heard my voice and smiled.

"Ruby, you look wonderful," he said as he walked over to me and shook my hand, "and you are walking so well. May I present Miss Angela Burdett Coutts, whom you have to thank for your situation."

The finely clad woman at the scarlet table nodded to me.

"I am pleased to meet you, Ruby," said Miss Coutts. Her voice was like a bird's, full of high grace, but warm. She rose and walked to the sofa, her petticoats rustling in a delicious cadence. "Charles, bring the girl over here. Standing on a gouty foot is hardly conducive to good conversation."

"I am very grateful to you indeed, Ma'am," I said as Dandy directed me to sit next her. "And I thank you for the dress, too."

"You are most welcome," she answered. "Mr. Dickens tells me that you are an experienced seamstress. Tell me, what do you hope to gain from your time here at the cottage?"

How the bloody hell should I know that? I just got here!

"To begin again, Ma'am," I said. Dickens winked from behind the sofa.

"I hope that you justify his faith in you," interjected Miss Coutts.

"I hope so too, Ma'am," I answered. I was fully aware that I was staring at her, and the expression on her face told me she knew it, too.

"What is it, my dear?" she asked.

"Forgive me for staring, Ma'am," I answered. "It's just that your dress is so exquisitely tailored. And the lace; I've never seen such intricate tatting."

"And where did you learn to appreciate the needle arts?"

"From my parents, Ma'am," I answered. "My father was a tailor and my mother a milliner. I used to look at the fashion magazines and try to see how make ladies clothes."

Miss Coutts smiled. "You are clever, aren't you? And you approve of my dress?"

"Yes. But if you'll forgive me for saying, tan gloves would suit you better than those white ones."

"Indeed?" laughed Miss Coutts.

"What did I tell you, Miss Coutts? By God, Mrs. Acton shall have competition before she knows it!" exclaimed Dandy.

"Ruby," said the Lady, "I should like, if you are able, to know something of how you came to your unfortunate circumstances."

Shit. I did not stir or speak.

"Surely you understand, my child, that we seek only to help you. Will you prove your trust of us by letting us in to your confidence?"

I looked at Dickens, still too hurt to speak.

"Ruby," he said as he knelt and took my hand in his, "This is what I was trying to say at the prison. It may help you to release the pain of such memories if you face them." His tone was not of demand, but the gentleness of a father to a child. Miss Coutts waited with silent grace, though her eyes never left my face.

"I don't mean no disrespect, Miss Coutts," I responded, "seeing as you're the one paying for all of this. I know you're a decent Lady, and I don't question your goodness. But—"

The words just stopped coming. I shook my head in resignation and stared back down at my lap. Dickens's hands still held mine; his right thumbnail had a speck of ink under it. I wished I could jump into the blue waves on my skirts and drown in them. But sink or swim, I couldn't run this time. So I decided whispering might be easier.

"My Pa..."

"A brute?" Miss Coutts asked.

"Don't you dare call him that!" I shouted. *That's right, Ruby. Scream at the rich Lady who gave you a place to live. Idiot!*

They both waited patiently. The fire cracked and spit while Rex answered it with chirps. I knew I had to tell them something. If I couldn't prove I trusted them, perhaps they would make me leave?

"I don't want to talk about this," I said.

"Charles," said Miss Coutts, "please leave us for a little while."

His eyes betrayed his outrage, but he obeyed.

"Please, Ruby," said the Lady once we were alone, "trust me."

*****

My pocket watch told me I had been pacing outside the parlour for fifteen minutes. My hunger to know the identity of who had defiled Ruby knew no bounds. The journalist in me would not be put off. So, I carefully pressed my ear to the door. Oh, why must women whisper?

"I ain't ashamed of living, Miss. But you and Mr. Dickens have done right by me. So I'll do my best to muck in and earn my keep. But, if you please, Ma'am, I won't answer no more questions."

I could imagine Miss Coutts placing her hands on Ruby's shoulders as she continued.

"Ruby, you are welcome here as long as you need to be here."

I knocked and heard Miss Coutts bid me enter. She was dabbing her eyes with an ivory silk handkerchief.

"Ruby," said she, "your trust means a great deal. Your courage and intelligence have held you this far. Let God's compassion touch them both, and you will thrive, I swear it."

I thought back to when had first met Ruby on that cold night in the shadow of Southwark Cathedral. She was an enigma to me from the beginning, in her words, her clothes, even in my arms. In prison she had been volatile, a volcano of a temper. Now, clad in the garments of a respectable woman, she was vulnerable, becoming an innocent child again in front of our eyes, yet haunted by the humiliation that had stripped her of human consolation. This was beautiful, and even in her sorrow, so was she.

"Thank you Ruby," said Miss Coutts, "now I should like some time to confer with Mr. Dickens in private."

"Very well," said Ruby, who answered as if she had been bred in a palace. I escorted her to the parlour door. She hardly limped at all anymore, and her posture was as straight as always. As I opened it for her, she turned to Miss Coutts.

"Shall I have some coffee sent in, Ma'am?"

Miss Coutts blinked once in surprise. Then her cheeks dappled as she responded, "Why thank you my dear, how very thoughtful. Good day, Ruby."

"Good luck, my girl," I said to Ruby.

Ruby smiled and curtseyed. Despite a slight wince, she did so as if she had been bred in a castle. "Good day, Miss Coutts. Mr. Dickens." Then she took her leave.

Miss Coutts rose and went back to the table. She rested her reticule on the scarlet cloth. From inside it, she took out a small notebook (she also made notes of the girls in the cottage) and began to write.

"I congratulate you, Charles," she said as she looked up from her writing, "Ruby is a remarkable girl. To have faced all of that alone, and to have retained her dignity. My God. Admirable strength."

I put my hands behind my back and proceeded toward the window once again.

"I take it she confided in you?"

"Yes. On the condition that I keep her secret to myself."

What?

I spun back around, "She does not trust me?"

"That, Charles, still remains to be seen."

Damn the writing, Charles. Think of what is best for Ruby! If this will help her, then so be it! You can get stories elsewhere and you know it. And you know you could never turn this girl away.

"Nevertheless, my dear Miss Coutts, we shall do our best for the girl."

Miss Coutts pursed her lips as she looked up at me, the twinkle in her eye told me she agreed. Then her gaze returned to her notebook. Outside, a chimney sweep was walking by with his donkey and cart. There was no way of determining which of the three was the most squalid.

But the air was cold and aside from them the street view was a bit sparse today. I turned my attention to the basket of ribbons on the other chair at the table. I picked it up and sat down, twirling their silky magnificence around my fingers.

My dabbles and battles with printers over the years had taught me to read type, which was set upside down and backwards. I twirled the ribbon around my finger and watched as Miss Coutts finished her notations: *Rubina Waller. Father in law bad.*

*****

By half past eight, I was ready to sleep in the coal shed if necessary. My limbs ached, all I wanted was to sleep. It felt odd to be tired not from walking endlessly or laying under Top, but from honest work. I had not felt that kind of fatigue in ages.

The daily duties seemed easy enough from what I had seen on my first day. But all this prayer was going to take getting used to. I had prayed before as a girl when my father was alive. But God had abandoned me to the hands of a brutal Step Father. Later, I was been reduced to no more than a street dog's bitch. God clearly had no use for me.

I sat there at the parlour table (I was excused from kneeling on account of my gouty foot) with my hands folded neatly on my skirts. I bowed my head and tried to set my face in the same demure manner that I had seen on the ladies in the fashion magazines. I feigned interest in the dulcet, meaningless words that issued from Mrs. Holdsworth's mouth, and answered when the other girls did. In short, I did as I was told, all the while hoping it would be over soon. It was no different than lying under a man, really. Come to think of it, prayer was a type of thievery, too, only in this game you hoped to distract God's attention from your sins by feigning penitence. The only thing missing were the thirty pieces of silver at our feet.

But Julia prayed fervently, her knuckles white from the ardent clasp of her hands. Every so often she would wrinkle her face to fight the falling of a tear, her attempt to prevent it usually in vain. Rosina also seemed deep in prayer.

Out of the lot who knelt there, it was only Mary Anne, who, hands steepled, wore an empty countenance on her face. She glanced at me, perhaps expecting to frighten me by the narrowing of her eyes. I did not look away from her gaze, and watched her boil on the inside because of it. Finally, she slowly drew in a very deep breath, let it out, and broke the stare. She had it in for me.

When prayers were ended, Julia led me up the steps to our room. It was at the end of the hall on the left. There were two beds neatly made, and the plaster walls were clean. A small hearth with a fire grate was in the wall opposite the beds, and a simply-sown pair of white curtains adorned the window, hanging down past the ledge.

A tiny vanity with a mirror was in the far corner, and it was dotted with a few hairbrushes and pins. There were also petite silver hair boxes; something I remember my mother using in order to stow hair from her brush to make into a new hairpieces. Since there were two, I knew one of them was to be mine.

Julia lit the fire, and directed me to the bed nearest the window. I collapsed gratefully upon it, and reached down toward my shoes.

"Mary Anne moved down the passage this morning, and I can't tell you how grateful I am, Ruby. You'll find nightclothes in the dresser. When you've changed, we'll bring our dresses to Mrs. Fisher."

"What for?" I asked as I paused with my shoes.

"Because all of our clothes get locked up at night. Mrs. H. says it's to prevent theft."

"Oh I see. A right tartar, isn't she? And all that business about the poor being blessed. What a load of rubbish."

"Ruby," said Julia in surprise, "how do you think you got here? God has seen fit to help you – all of us."

"Well what took him so bloody long? That's what I'd like to know."

Just as she was about to answer, the door opened, and Mary Anne sped in. She was already clad in her night clothes, her mousy hair lose about her sparse shoulders.

"Forgot me brush," she uttered walking over to the dresser, nearly knocking Julia over who was setting the warming pan down ready for the coals.

"Easy, Mary Anne," I said. "You'll send Julia into the fire that way."

Mary Anne whirled around from retrieving her brush on the dresser.

"Oh, well I do beg your pardon, Your Ladyship," she intoned, and bowed in defiance. "Here one bleeding day and already barking orders? Oh that's right, I forgot. You're D.'s new favorite wench."

I stared at her. "How dare you."

She took a few steps closer and picked up my shoe from the floor. "I do dare, hussy."

"Mary Anne," said Julia, "if I had your nerve in a tooth, I'd pull it out by the root."

Mary Anne flashed Julia a look of warning. "And if you want to hang on to your own, keep out of my way." Then she turned back to me. "Course, it ain't your mouth he's interested in, or is it?" She raised the tip of my shoe to her mouth and licked it. "That how you got in here, slut?"

I shot up onto my feet and clutched my shoe from out of her child-sized paw. My small frame towered nearly half a head above Mary Anne. Her grip tightened around the brush, and she began to raise it over her head.

"Girls, don't," said Julia firmly.

I did not heed her. I merely stared down at the pair of desperate, soulless eyes that were fixed upon mine. Just at that moment soft footsteps came down the passage, and there was a knock on the door.

"Girls," Mrs. Fisher's voice rang out, "time to turn in your clothes. No dawdling."

Mary Anne lowered the brush, spat at my feet, wiped her nose on her hand, and walked out. It had taken all my strength not only to stand barefoot on that cold floor, but to maintain that posture exhausted what little energy I had. The moment the door slammed shut and Mrs. Fisher's voice called out to Mary Anne not to slam doors, I sank back to the bed and exhaled a long breath I hadn't known I had held.

"Christ," I sighed, "my poor pins." All I wanted was sleep. I longed to let my hair down, brush it, and settle in between the sheets of my new bed.

"Ruby," said Julia as she walked over to the dresser and took out a nightdress, "don't let her get you. She's been trouble since she got here. Here, I'll help you."

"Ta. And you're right of course, Julia," I answered, steeling myself to stand again. I swung my skirt over my head, and she began to help me out of my corset. "Still, if she tries it ever again, I'll pound the bitch through the floorboards."

CHAPTER XIII

RUBY DREAMS OF THE BADGER GAME, AND WHAT WAS TO COME.

I was sitting on Top's lap the night he told me. As he did most nights, he had told me a story before I went to sleep.

"Do genies really exist, Top?"

"Of course," he said whimsically as he tapped my nose with his fingertip, "just like faeries do."

I giggled. I fancied being a magical faerie.

"I am a Genie of sorts, you know," said Top.

I looked at him in wonder, "No you aren't."

"I am. A man hurt you. Hurt you in your cunny."

I closed my eyes and turned into his chest, "No! I don't want to remember that."

"If your wish is revenge," said Top. "I would gladly grant it, my lamb."

I began to cry with shame, "I'm too small to hurt anyone."

Top placed his hand under my chin. "Nonsense, Child. Why, you are the perfect size. Everything about you is perfect. Aye! A vengeful faerie is a thing to behold."

"What do you mean?" I asked as I looked up at him.

"What say you of men, my little faerie?"

"I hate them," I spat as much venom as a ten year old can possess.

"And me?" he asked.

"No, I don't hate you."

He kissed my forehead. "Would you like to humiliate them? Would you like to make them pay?" he whispered into my hair.

I looked up at him. "How?"

"Talk to them," he said simply. "I shall do the rest."

"But—"

"Do I not always keep you safe?" said Top, sensing my hesitation.

"Yes."

The game was as easy for me as breathing. Talk to the gentleman, take his arm and walk with the gentleman, smile – don't forget to smile. And laugh; they like that. Lead them 'round into the alley. Then Top would appear.

"That's my daughter! You villain! You monster! She is but eight years old. I'll summon the Peelers!"

The man's face turns to linen. "I beg of you, Sir. Spare me!"

"My daughter's honour is now in question, you savage. I demand reparation."

"Anything."

"What shall you pay?"

"Anything!"

And so our nights went in this strange theatre. Fabrics and dolls were showered upon me. For two years, this was our arrangement. Mousie tolerated my presence and Collette hardly looked at me. I was never asked to lift a finger in housework. My time was spent reading and altering dresses to my liking.

The day I reached twelve years of age, everything changed. It was the legal age of consent. That night, Top asked if he might make love to me. I did not agree out of any obligation. I agreed because the way he touched me made my flesh sing.

"Did you like it, Ruby?" panted Top. He rested on his elbows above me, sweat glistening on his skin. His eyes bore an expression I remember a Reverend once had after a booming sermon. He had worn a French Letter of sheepgut.

"Oh, Top." The words formed on my lips, but I could not speak. A feeling had built inside me until I thought I would piss the bed. But instead, every muscle in my body shattered, wept, screamed, and laughed—all in a single instant. It was to be the first time of many.

"Aphrodite herself is folly compared to your beauty," continued my lover. "You have found your wings, my faerie. I worship you. Oh God, I cannot be without you."

He continued to kiss my neck as he lay, still atop me, still inside my quivering sheath. That was how my training had begun. The men he found for me were always to wear French Letters, or Safes. A ready supply was on in my nightstand, along with vinegar water, just to be certain.

The tip of my nose was cold when I woke. For a moment I thought I was still at Tothill Fields, and forgot I had a good pair of slippers just below on the floor waiting to receive me.

It wasn't until I opened my eyes and beheld Julia brushing her hair at the small corner table that I remembered I was in a new home. I was no longer in that bloody awful infirmary. Today, Doctor Wilkins would not be paying me one of his daily visits. The memory of his kiss upon my hand made chest felt heavy for a moment.

"Good morning Ruby," said Julia, wearing a blue wrapper. She smiled at my face in the mirror and chirped with morning energy as great as Rex's.

"Up with you now. Prayers in ten minutes. And breakfast won't cook itself. Look sharp, or Mrs. H. will have both our heads."

I thought of Collette's severed head. I yawned to cover up the shiver.

"Fine. I'll be ready in a moment. Nice little room, this."

Julia giggled and brought the brush to her mouth. "Isn't it lovely in the sunlight? Ruby, I hope you and I shall be good pals."

I donned my slippers and the green wrapper she had left at the foot of my bed the night before, and walked to the window. When I parted the curtains the warm welcoming sun blazed its greeting onto my face and into my eyes. I found myself wondering for the first time what made the sun so warm. Was it made of fire? How could it be up in the sky if it was? I laughed at my new found sense of philosophy.

"What's so funny?" asked Julia, who was pouring warm water into the Wedgewood bowl on the washstand which stood on the other side of our window.

"Nothing," said I, and walked over to her. A cake of lavender soap sat on the side of the stand, its crisp bouquet like a siren's call. I took the soap in hand and gently plunged my arms into with the basin. The lather was sweet on my skin. Even a princess could not have enjoyed that more than I did.

Morning prayers were just as meaningless as the evening ones had been. All I could think about was breakfast. A full belly was far more valuable than a clean soul as far as I could see. I entered the kitchen to find the work table cluttered with a large brown butter crock, a plate of cold ham, and a coffee grinder. Upon the hob sat a pot with gently rolling water. Rosina was bent over it, stirring. From the smell, I knew it was porridge.

"Morning, girls," said Rosina as she shook the end of the spoon on the lip of the kettle before replacing the lid. Julia and I returned her greeting just as Mrs. Holdsworth entered. From what I had seen, her sense of color seemed to be as blind as Dandy's, something I would not have thought possible. Her dark purple striped housecoat did not become her at all. The stripes were far too wide for her frame. The white cap gave her the appearance of a frost-laden bunch of dying grapes.

"Well, Ruby," she said, "I am indeed glad to see that you are punctual. Now set to work; get some water for coffee. Then help with the toast."

"Yes, Ma'am," I answered, and began rummaging around the kitchen.

Later, everyone dressed in practical clothes, as we had a day full of chores and lessons ahead. Breakfast was a spread of porridge, toast, eggs and ham. After the food at Tothill Fields, tucking in to a good breakfast was a delight sweeter than any sermon.

According to the list, Rosina and I were to work together today. She had a head of curly, auburn hair that definitely preferred to think for itself. Even drawn back in a topknot, several tendrils defiantly hung loose about her house cap, refusing to be ordered about. Her simple dark green dress provided the perfect complement to her hair and lightly freckled skin. She was taller than me by about eight inches. Her hands were slender and tapered; perfect for the life of a pickpocket.

We went into the kitchen where she showed me the great copper tub and scrub board located near the larder. We brought that out along with cakes of soap and strung up several drying lines from one wall to the other. Then she placed a large kettle on the hob and I filled it with jug after jug of water from the pump sink.

As we did all this, the girls fetched sheets, chemises, stockings, nightdresses, dresses, tablecloths, napkins aprons and anything else that needed a scrub. They arrived with four full baskets. I soaked and scrubbed the garments at the wash board until they practically begged for reprieve. My arms throbbed from the exertion. My knuckles were red and swollen.

I'd rather they be this way from rendering Mary Anne's face unrecognizable.

Rosina and I managed to work out a system. I would scrub, we would wring out. Then she hung the wet clothes on the rack. The hob fire cast its warmth like a thick street fog, and the room soon took on the glow and feel of a baker's shop at summer noontime.

Fortunately, I found that Rosie was as chatty as I was, and since Mrs. Holdsworth detested morning wash, we were left in the company of Mrs. Fisher. That suited me right down to the ground.

Mrs. Fisher, to my delight but not to my surprise, rolled up her sleeves. She fetched more water with no airs at all. Then she took the chair next to me. In her simple brown and red woolen dress, she was plain and stout-looking; more like one of us than assistant matron. After she was certain we knew what we were doing, she dried her arms and sat at the kitchen table, working on that afternoon's reading lesson.

"How's Rex this morning, Kit—um, Mrs. F.?" I asked as I stood to stretch.

"He is fine, I'm sure," she answered. "I don't normally look in on him until later."

"I want to feed him again today," said Rosina, and whistled.

I drew up my apron with my hands and began to fan myself.

"Only if I get to as well, Rosie," said I as I sat back down and reached for the soap.

"Well if we keep on schedule today, perhaps you can feed him crumbs after tea," said Mrs. Fisher as she rose. "You look like you know what you are doing here, and I must go see how the other girls are getting on."

A loud crash came from the parlour, swiftly followed by swearing and what sounded like furniture being knocked about.

"Oh dear," said Mrs. Fisher, who promptly exited the room.

"Always wanted a bird," said Rosie.

"What," I asked, "like them rich toffs have?"

"Yeah, and sailors, too," said Rosie.

The memory of my disastrous encounters with that monster of a harpooner made me drop the soap near the hearth.

"Ruby, you feeling poorly?" asked Rosie, who knelt down to pick up the soap. She held on to my hand a bit longer than I felt necessary.

"No," I said, "Now drop my hand before I break your arm."

"Didn't mean anything. Honest!" continued Rosie. *Do I still have a fever, or is she looking at me the way Wilkins did? Top told me about girls like this.*

I squared my shoulders.

"Rosie, I don't need anything. Now let go of my hand. I don't plan on being stuck in here all day with the likes of you."

"I—I didn't mean anything, Ruby," Rosie quickly said.

"You think I care? Well then, you're a fool. Let's finish the wash and forget about it. But if you touch me again, I'll shove your head in this tub and wait for the bubbles to stop coming up."

Rosie nodded. I did not speak to her for the rest of the day.

CHAPTER XIV

SOUP, SEWING, AND STRANGE SITUATIONS.

"Well if they are the less fortunate," I asked as I wiped my eyes with my forearm, "I should like to know what the hell that makes us, then?"

A stern look for Mrs. Holdsworth ended the giggles of contemplation as we prepared more vegetables, scraps and peels for the newly simmering water in the soup pot. We frequently made soup out of leftover food for the poor—nothing was to be wasted. Today it was my lot to do the onions. They, like many a man, were having their way with me.

"Sorry Mrs. H.," I said, "But I must own that soup making ain't my idea of fun."

"*Is not* my idea of fun," corrected Mrs. H. "And it is high time that you—" she said, then further gesticulated to include the other girls, "all of you, did something charitable. Unless you find yourself still too frail for a task as simple as making soup, Ruby?"

My expression folded into one of guarded contempt. "Not at all, Ma'am," I answered in as flat a voice as I could.

She cast one more look of disdain in our direction, and left the kitchen. As had become our secret custom after one of Mrs. H.'s stern lectures, we turned and curtsied in unison to the now closed door. Then, still and silent, we listened for the telltale sound of the parlour door being shut.

"Funny," said Rosie, as she rubbed her cunny with the handle of the spoon, "I have always thought of myself as being very charitable, indeed!"

The room erupted into fits of choking and sputtering as we tried to muffle our laughter.

"Jesus, she do think highly of us lot, don't she?" said Rosie twirling the spoon and prancing about the table. "Needs a good fuck if you ask me."

"What, her?" I asked, "That old dragon wouldn't know what to do if she had one!"

A knock at the door forced us to contain ourselves.

"Ruby," said Mrs. Fisher, her cap and curls wriggling like Mr. Punch's baby as she spoke, "you have a visitor in the parlour."

"Thank you, Mrs. Fisher," I answered, and dashed to the sink and began to scrub my hands and arms with soap and brush.

"Who do you think it is?" asked Julia excitedly.

"Don't care in the least," I said as I scrubbed, "but anything's better than slicing these bloody onions."

I was tidy in three minutes, and I made my way to the parlour. When I opened the door, I saw Mr. Dickens feeding Rex a bit of a stale scone.

"Ah," he said, dropping the crust into Rex's cage and gesturing for me to sit on the sofa, "there you are. How are you faring, my dear?"

"I ain't your dear, Dandy," said I as I gave him a wry smile and sat down, "And unless you have a nip of gin and a cigarette hanging about your person, I have work to do."

"Forgive me, I had no idea you were so fond of cutting onions," he remarked with a sniff. "Use lemon juice next time. And why are you being so terse with me?" he inquired with an eyebrow raised.

"Because I know why you're here."

"Indeed? Well, enlighten me, Ruby. Why am I here?" he asked. His manner never ceased to amaze me. He was the most fidgety man I had ever met, but also the most fluid. He sat down next to me with the ease and grace of Napoleon himself.

"You want me to tell you about my life," I said, staring into the fire, "And I said I didn't want to."

"I am sorry to surprise you, but that was not the reason for my visit, Ruby."

"What, then?" I asked as I turned to look at him, "I ain't in trouble, am I?"

He laughed. "No. But I did want to ask you something."

"Go ahead," said I.

"What would you say to a commission?" asked Dickens.

"Depends on what it is. And knowing your imagination, I—"

"I would like you to make a dress for one of my daughters," he interrupted.

"Have you her measurements?" I said, attempting to sound as unimpressed as I possibly could just to spite him.

"I do not."

I shrugged and stood up, "Can't help you, then. Now if you will excu—"

"I am aware of that you need the measurements, Ruby," said Dandy as he gently took my arm and sat me back down. "You shall come to my home and take them."

"What's that?" I said. My heart began to beat in a panic, but I wasn't sure why.

"Well, I cannot very well bring her here, now can I?"

"And why not, may I ask? Ain't, I mean, aren't we fit to be seen yet?"

"Hardly," answered Dickens. "This is not a fit place for a little girl."

"What the hell is that supposed to mean?" I said as I glared at him, "That's all you've got here is a house full of little girls. We're all young, except for Mrs. H."

"I meant only that your education is not yet complete," he answered. "However, this will be a good experience for you, and your pay shall be held in trust until your time here is completed." He stood and walked to the parlour door.

"A hansom shall call for you tomorrow morning at eleven o'clock."

I whirled about on my knees and glared at him from over the back of the sofa, "Hang on, I haven't accepted the commission yet!"

"Then I look forward to being surprised tomorrow, one way or another. Good day, Ruby."

When I returned to the kitchen my blood was fit to boil as well as that damned soup was.

"Well, well. Invited to the Master's house. I wonder what other plans he's got," said Mary Anne, leaning in the doorway.

"A crass little cunt like you would have her mind in the gutter," I said as I walked past her.

"Say that again," I heard her exclaim from behind me.

"Are you deaf as well as daft?" I said as I turned to face Mary Anne, who was now right next to me at the stove.

"You're one to talk of gutters, Ruby," said Mary Anne with a sneer, "Ain't that where he found you?"

I thrust the ladle back into the pot hard enough for the soup to splash on her arm. She jumped back, burned left forearm covered by her right hand. Her eyes glistened with hate.

"Fuck off," I growled lowly.

Again I heard that distinct clicking of Mary Anne's tongue as she left the room.

"Ruby," exclaimed Julia, "I told you, don't ruffle her—"

"Stow it, Julia," I said, rather shortly. "I can take care of myself. I've done it long enough."

"I only want to help," she whispered, on the verge of tears. Truth be told, she was regularly on the verge of tears—especially when she prayed, which was often. The other girls often teased her, and said that she spent more time on her knees than the rest of us had.

"Julia, I'm sorry," I said as I embraced her, "but I'll be damned if she's going to get the better of me. I won't let her win."

"Win what?" asked my compatriot as she handed me my apron.

"Whatever game she's playing, Julia," I answered as I put the lid on the soup pot.

*****

"Charles, you cannot be serious!" ejaculated Catherine from her chair. Normally when she remonstrated with me she would pace or follow me about. But this time, her middle bulging with another Dickens, she remained seated.

"I am perfectly serious, Catherine," I answered, "Miss Waller is an excellent seamstress. Furthermore, she is worthy of the commission."

"But Charles, she is—"

"She is what, Catherine? Come now, if you are going to intimate something, say it."

"She, she is—"

"A whore," I interjected. "I believe that is the word you cannot say, is it not?"

"Yes, Charles," she answered. Her eyes were blinking rapidly. Whether the cause was embarrassment or frustration, I could not read.

"Correction, Catherine. She was a whore. Now she is not. Her past is not to be spoken of."

"But Charles, it is only that—"

"I said the past is not spoken of."

"I understand and agree that that is best, Charles. Please believe me when I say that I do not judge the poor creature. I am certain she had no choice in her fate. But may I ask you one question more?"

"Of course you may."

"I am sure this girl is very dear, but what are we to tell Katey?"

"Tell Katey the truth. Miss Waller is a friend who is very poor and in need of work. Will that do?"

"Admirably, Charles," she said. Then she looked over to me at smiled, "Thank you."

"For what?"

"For giving this girl a chance," she said sweetly.

I knelt before my wife's chair and smiled at her. Moments like this one made our more disagreeable ones fade quickly. I leaned in and kissed her.

"What else could I do?" I said, my forehead touching hers.

"You really cannot help yourself, can you?"

"You know me too well," said I as I kissed her again. Her eyes were alight like twinkling stars, and I placed my hand on hers and felt our child move.

"He is restless," I observed.

"Terribly," my wife returned.

I put my lips to her swollen middle and kissed it.

"You in there," I said softly, "Let you poor mother get some sleep. There's a good little chap."

"Perhaps a Lass, Charles," said Catherine as she put her hand around my neck. She kissed my head. I closed my eyes and savored the emotion.

Even a man of letters can recognize and treasure those times when words are completely unnecessary.

CHAPTER XV

OLD FRIENDS MEET AGAIN.

It was market day. Today, it was to be our classroom. Mrs. F. brought some of us out to see how well we could keep accounts on household spending. It was close to Christmas; soon the shops and market stalls would sing with decoration and swim with produce.

It was my job to purchase a suitable turkey. The butcher was a great hulking man, with forearms like Goliath. As I stood there looking at the enormous array of dead birds, their featherless bodies hanging loose and ashamed, a man walked up very close to me, and put his hand on my arm. I thought perhaps it was a test Mrs. Holdsworth had cooked up, so I answered like I thought a Lady would.

"Sir, kindly desist. Or I shall summon the police."

"I mean you no harm. Be quiet and listen. Pretend to gesture to different birds as if I'm helping you select one."

I glanced over at him. It was the cab driver who had brought me to Urania!

"You're the cabbie," I said.

"I am more than that. You don't remember me. I don't blame you for blocking it all from your mind. Many's the time I have tried to as well. How could I expect you to remember back to when you were little? You don't even remember that night in the Thames, do you?"

Suddenly, I did remember. *Those eyes. That voice!*

"You saved my life!" I said with a smile as I pointed to a goose.

"I am trying to do it again now. Do you want Top to find you?"

My hand shook as I pointed to a very large turkey.

"What?" I exclaimed, my reticle nearly slid off my arm as I brought it back down in a hurry.

"You didn't see Mary Anne shuffle off behind the bread stall, did you? Know who she's talking to? Get out of Urania, Ruby."

"Why should I?"

"Top means you harm, Child. I have it on good authority."

I faced the young man now.

"Who's?"

"A little mouse told me."

I understood his meaning. "Mousie," I said.

"Aye," said the man, "I know you. I can't explain now, but we've a common past. I will do my best to protect you, Ruby. But I hope you heed my warning."

"But I can't just up and leave," I argued.

"Find a way."

The handsome young man kissed my cheek as if I were a cherished sister, and walked away.

"Ruby," said Mrs. Fisher, "what was that young man saying to you?"

"Oh I asked him to help me pick out the best turkey of the bunch," I answered. "Wasn't very helpful, though."

CHAPTER XVI

RUBY VISITS NO. 1 DEVONSHIRE TERRACE, WHERE THE PAST IS SEEMLINGLY NEVER FAR AWAY.

No. 1 Devonshire Terrace was as posh as I thought it would be. Tiled floors, plush green draperies, gilded mirrors, carpets of brilliant colors and above all, light. It was all the things I expected from Dandy. Opulent and glittering, it was a house to be envied by a prince.

The maid took my bonnet and cloak and I was shown into the drawing room to meet Mrs. Dickens, who was sat upon the sofa of a deep claret. There were already fabrics laid on the nearby chair, presumably for us to choose from for her daughter's dress.

Mrs. Dickens very pleasant enough to the eye; her dark auburn hair shone from under her fine linen house cap. She was nearing the end of her confinement, her bulge quite pronounced from under her dark grey silk house coat. The lace tucker at her neck looked like a cloud perched upon her breast. The mother of so many children, her figure was understandably a bit plump. But her face, framed by lovely, shining cheeks, reflected a kindness my mother had never shown me. All in all, I thought Mrs. Dickens very comely, indeed.

However, as soon as she saw me, her smiled melted. Her enchanting, drooping eyelids snapped up like soldiers to battle. Two blue pools shone at me with an intensity I did not think such a Genteel Lady was capable of.

"How do you do, Mrs. Dickens?" I said as I curtsied.

She blinked several times, as if I had greeted her in some foreign, heathen tongue. Then she came to her senses. "Very well, thank you, Miss Waller," she responded. "You are most welcome here. Pray, be seated."

"Thank'ee, Ma'am," I said and sat in the chair she gestured to with her lace-mitted hand. A proper coffee had been laid on a table which sat just in front of and slightly to the right of my hostess. It smelled much better than the stuff at the Home. The china was very fine, accompanied by pressed linen napkins and silver spoons—anyone of which I could have used as a looking glass.

"I must ask you to forgive my initial greeting of you, Miss Waller," said Mrs. Dickens.

"Not at all, Mrs. Dickens," said I, thinking her delicate condition as the cause, "I quite underst—"

"No, Miss Waller," interrupted Mrs. Dickens, "you do not. Mr. Dickens has informed me that you are from Urania Cottage."

"I see," I said as I cast my eyes at the exquisite rug beneath our feet.

Mrs. Dickens held out her hand to draw my face up again. "Please, I would never wish to infer that I judge you or your past," she said apologetically, "I am certain your dressmaking skills are more than adequate, else Mr. Dickens would not have requested this audience."

"That's kind of you, Ma'am," I said, "And, if you please, I would be obliged if you were to call me Ruby. I know it isn't proper like, but I have more of a tolerance for my Christian name."

"Well, if it will make you feel more comfortable, then Ruby it shall be. Katey will join us soon. I think she will like you."

"I look forward to meeting the little'un, Missus," I said, "Mr. Dickens says she's a keen little artist."

"Yes, she takes after me," said Mrs. Dickens with a wink, "Will you take some coffee, my dear?"

"Thank you, yes. Oh, shall I pour? How do you take it?" I said, rising from my seat, "You shouldn't be leaning over just now, Missus, if you don't mind my saying so."

Mrs. Dickens laughed again and patted her middle, "My, but you do like to feel at home, don't you? Thank you, Ruby. Milk and sugar, please, dear. Tell me, how do you like the Cottage?"

"Well," I said as the silver pot yielded a rich and delicious ebony stream, "it's never a bore, Ma'am. They keep us busy and the place is very tidy…"

I kept talking as I finished preparing our coffees and sat back down. All the while, I could feel her eyes on me.

"Is something wrong, Missus?" I inquired as kindly as politely as I knew how.

"No," she laughed, though this giggle was of a nervous bent, "Forgive me for staring, Miss—Ruby. It is only that you remind me—"

I finished a sip, "What's that, Missus?"

"It is only that you remind me of someone," she answered.

"Really?" I asked as I stirred the coffee with my spoon, trying to remember not to let it clank against the cup, "Who?"

Mrs. Dickens hesitated, her face drained of joy again. Then, her eyes grew wet. I thought at first that she was going to weep, but only a few small tears fell. I have often heard that women who are in their confinement are prone to rapid change of emotions. It was when she turned her head away from me that I started to worry.

"Are you quite well, Ma'am?" I asked in case she was ill.

She drew in a deep breath and turned around to face me. Her mouth opened as if she were going to say something. But she was interrupted by an unexpected knock at the door. Dandy made a speedy entrance into our midst with a fetching little girl in tow who was the image of him.

Out of the corner of my eye, I saw Mrs. Dickens's eyes burn as she beheld her husband. I began to wonder just what the hell I had gotten myself into. Beneath the sparkling finery, a dark secret loomed within these walls. And somehow, I was a part of it.

*****

With an excited Katey by my side, I entered the drawing room to find Ruby taking coffee with Catherine. The sofa and nearby chairs were awash in different fabrics.

My daughter stood transfixed as she beheld Ruby. Suddenly she smiled as bright as the sun and ran into Ruby's arms shouting, "It's you! It's really you!"

"Who, Katey?" asked my wife.

"It's the lilac fairy!" my daughter exclaimed.

"What's that, dearie?" inquired Ruby, who was just as shocked as Catherine.

"You are the one that Papa told us about; the one he met that night during his walk. I drew a likeness of you," my daughter stayed in Ruby's embrace as she looked back at me, "It is her, isn't it Papa? She's wearing lilac ribbons in her hair. I knew she was real, and you have brought her to me. Oh thank you, Papa!"

Ruby looked over at me with a look of bewilderment on her face.

"Katey, my darling," said Catherine as she held out her hand to our daughter, "what on earth are you—"

"Is your name really Ruby?" said Katey to Ruby, so excited that she did not even hear her mother speaking.

"Yes."

"Just like the jewel! It's a beautiful name."

"Thank'ee kindly, Miss," said Ruby.

"Are you going to make a dress for me?" asked the child.

"Aye."

"Wonderful!" exclaimed my daughter whimsically as she climbed up and sat in between the two women. "Mama, may I help select the fabric? Please?"

"Of course you may, darling," replied my wife.

"I was unaware that fairies make dresses, Miss Ruby," said Katey. Without giving Ruby time to respond, Katey turned her attention to her mother, "Ha—I wonder what else they do, Mama!"

Catherine set her drooping eyelids dead upon me.

"So do I," she said.

CHAPTER XVII

WHEN SECRETS ARE UNLOCKED, CONFRONTATIONS WILL INEVITABLY FOLLOW.

"Miss," I said to Katey, "please hold still now. Don't want to make a pin cushion out of you, dearie."

"Sorry," said Katey.

"Oh I don't really mind," I reassured her as I tugged at the light copper-coloured fabric, "I always get excited about new dresses, too!"

"How did you meet Papa?" the child asked.

I coughed.

"Well, um, your Papa likes to walk—and so do I. That's how we met. I was out for a walk. He was out for a walk—"

"You were out for a walk at night time? Oh, you are very brave, Miss Ruby. Girls aren't supposed to walk at night. But then again, I suppose you can use your magic to keep you safe!"

"Ah, yes. Exactly so, Miss Katey."

She began to fidget again.

"What is it now, dearie? You need to get rid of that milk you drank?"

She giggled, "No. I—I was just wondering if—"

Her eyes, as bright as her father's, were wide with wonder as she turned to face me.

"May—May I please see your wings?"

I dropped the pin cushion. "Come again?"

"Your wings. Papa said you have wings."

I put the pin cushion on the table and stood up to stretch.

"Oh, he did? I mean, he did. Yes, of course he did! Right. Um—"

"Please, may I see them, Miss Ruby? I promise I won't tell anyone. I want to compare them to the drawing I did of you. It would help to improve my shading technique."

"Oh, I see. Right, my wings. Well, you see, dear, they're—they're tucked under my corset just now. I do that during the day. Keeps them out of the way, you know. Only need them at night so I can fly around safely."

"Oh," she breathed, "I didn't think of it like that."

I smiled and patted her head.

"Now, turn around again, please, my Little Miss. I am almost finished."

The child obeyed. For about thirty seconds.

"Miss Ruby?"

"Yes?" I said carefully, the right corner of my mouth now full of pins.

"Do Faeries talk to Angels?"

I paused.

"Um, I think so." *How the hell should I know? All I want to do is finish this bloody hem!*

"Do you know any angels?"

I rose and helped her off the chair she had been standing on.

"Only one I see around here is you, sweet girl."

She giggled, "Thank you. I'll bet Papa mistook you for an Angel when he met you. You're the very image of Aunt Mary."

Hang on. Mary? That's the name Dickens said that night we spent together.

Katey continued her explanation without my having to ask.

"Papa thought her an Angel; I heard him say so once to Mama. She died ten years ago."

"Darling," I asked, "who was Mary?"

"One of Mama's younger sisters," Katey answered.

"Really? What else do you know about her?"

"Well, she died at our old house in Doughty Street. That's the house where I was born. I don't know exactly what happened, but she suddenly became ill and then she died. She and Papa were very good friends. You look very much like her, Miss Ruby. Papa wears her ring. He keeps a lock of her hair, too, and he put all of her clothes into a trunk…"

"I see. Well, I shall keep my eye out for that particular angel. Sounds like we have much to talk about, what with us both being friends of your Papa. By the by, Miss, what was Mary's surname?"

"Hogarth."

The pendant on his watch chain—C.D. to M.H. Mary Hogarth! Dandy, you liar. You good for nothing son of a bitch. Is that why you were so interested in me? I cannot wait to hear the tale you will craft to escape this one.

Miss Georgina opened the door.

"Time for tea, Katey."

"May Miss Ruby please join us, Aunt Georgy?"

Aunt? Come to think of it, now I see the resemblance to Katey's mother. How many Hogarth sisters have you kept under one roof, Dickens?

I helped Katey out of the pinned dress and slipped her own back on her.

"Perhaps the next time I visit. Right now, I must finish your new dress. You run along."

"I look forward to seeing you again soon," said Katey.

"So do I. Good day, Ladies."

"Good day, Miss," they both answered.

They left the room and I collapsed on the sofa. I shook with fury. I wanted to throw the dress in the fire, smash every vase and delicate thing in the room, rip down the drapes...

Perhaps that man who spoke to me at market was right. Perhaps I should leave Urania Cottage...

I decided to finish Katey's dress as I thought what next to do. Two hours later, the last of the trim had been added to the collar. It was finished. I packed up the sewing basket and laid the dress tenderly across the sofa and went into the large foyer. Dickens's study was nearby, that much I knew. I saw a light under one of the doors. I took a deep breath, walked across the tiled floor, and knocked.

"Who is it?" inquired Dickens.

"It's Ruby," I said as steadily as I could.

"Come in, dear girl."

Dickens sat at his desk in his shirtsleeves. The middle of the top portion of the desk was raised and slanted to make writing easier. He did not look up.

"Ah, there you are, my dear. You haven't finished already, have you?"

"Yes," I said, "I have finished. Both with the dress and with you.

"What?" he asked absent mindedly. He reached for another sheet of paper and continued to write. *You are not even listening to me!*

When I slammed my hand down on the paper, he looked at me as if I had just shot his children.

"Ruby, how dare you! I have a deadline!"

"You're good at stories, aren't you. Or should I say lies. You kept something from me, Dickens."

"Ruby, for God's sake, what are you—?"

I turned to face him.

"I'm not Ruby, Charles. I'm Mary. Isn't this what you want?"

He was paralyzed. "Ruby. How did you—?"

"Slipped your mind to tell me I look like a dead woman you loved, did it?"

"Ruby, please," he begged, hands raised in supposition, "do not do this."

"That's not who I am to you. You want me to be her, don't you? Call me Mary."

"No."

I began to undress.

"Do it, goddamn you," I ordered.

"I will not," he returned shakily, his jaw set.

The dress fell to the floor, and I stood in my corsets before him.

"Coward," I said as I spat at his feet.

He rushed at me, and held me tight by the arms.

"Stop this!" he ordered, "Stop it now!"

"Why," I questioned, breathless as I grabbed his hips and put them against mine, "we're just getting to the fun part. So, shall we to bed now, my darling Charles, or would you rather
mount me on your desk right here?"

His eyes narrowed as he released me with such force that I fell back against his desk.
"How dare you desecrate her memory in this way. I will not tolerate it! Get your own things back on this instant."

"I told you I take orders from no man."

"Do it at once!" he bellowed.

"You deceiving bastard. Your wife damn near had apoplexy when she saw me for the first time. Was that part of your miserable little game, too? Don't you care about anyone but yourself?"

"Silence," he sneered like a king.

"Oh shut up. You don't frighten me."

"Obey or I shall be forced to summon the police."

"Go on, then. I'm sure they'd like to hear how you went for me."

I tore my petticoats in defiance. He grabbed me by both wrists again. I broke free, but fell to the carpet.

"Get dressed," he said, his voice suddenly weary. His shoulders were curved forward; his eyes still ablaze with fury. Whether he was about to cry or strike me, I could not tell. But he did not move.

"You mind what you're about, Dandy. Send for the Peelers and I will tell what happened here tonight, you may lay to that!"

"You think I do not know that? It was always your intent to use me, was it not?"

"Likewise, I'm sure."

"Girl, you are mistaken."

I rose from the floor.

"Not to worry, Dandy. I'll solve the problem for both of us," said I as I donned my cloak. "Don't you dare follow me. Don't you dare try to find me. That's the price of my silence. It's over. Goodbye."

And so I left him there, alone, with my clothes. Hell, none of the garments were really mine, anyway. I walked for a few minutes, then hailed a cab.

"Where to, Miss?" the driver inquired. He saw my attire and gave me a puzzled look.

"Burton Crescent, Bloomsbury," I said. "The Gentleman I'm going to see will pay you handsomely for speed."

The driver did not disappoint. But at the corner of Russell Square, the horse leapt to a halt. I opened the window and looked out. A coal wagon had collided with a large wagon full of vegetables. Several people looked to be injured. One of the horses was lying in the middle of the cobbles. Agonized whinnies swirled with its hot breath, and gave the creature the appearance of a dragon awaiting the death blow from a knight of old.

This is my chance.

I curled my right hand around the handle of the carriage door and opened it as deftly as I could. I bundled my petticoats into my left hand, and slipped out as thread which rejects the needle's eye.

As if the heavens were inclined to echo my rage, thunder blasted like canon fire as I ran down

Guilford Street, then turned left on Marchmont. I was now only seconds away from Burton Crescent. I reached the elegantly curved row of brick houses; the street lamps barely afforded me any guidance. Rain began to fall. Breathless and shivering, I knocked on a door and hoped I had remembered the number correctly. The door opened, and the light from a very small whale oil lamp floated as a phantom in the darkened doorway. The tin reflector on the back of the lamp obscured the face of the person holding it. At first, they did not move or speak. I tried to think of an explanation for standing on a stranger's doorstep on a dark night in my petticoats that wouldn't warrant summoning the Peelers. But I needn't have worried.

"Ruby?"

"Yes. May I come in, Dr. Wilkins? Please?"

CHAPTER XVIII

RUBY FINDS SHELTER.

"Ruby," whispered Wilkins, the shock evident in his eyes at the sight of me.

"May I come in?" I repeated, trying to keep my teeth from chattering.

Wilkins blinked and shook his head as if he were willing himself to come out of a trance. Then, he moved aside and gestured for me to enter.

"My God, you're shivering, girl."

"Yes, well it is bloody f—fucking freezing outs—side."

Wilkins put his arm around me, walked me up to his flat. The long banyan he wore fitted his broad frame perfectly. The paisley designed fabric was a rust color that suited him right down to the ground. His flat was modest, but very neat. There were a few lithographs of ships on the walls, along with some other bizarre medical images that I had no desire to understand.

He sat me down in a dark leather wingback chair, and dashed out to pay the cabbie. Upon returning, he pulled another chair close to me for himself, and removed my bonnet. He put his hands on mine, which until then had been clutching my cloak about me, and pried them apart.

"Christ, Ruby, where the hell are your clothes?" I saw fear flash across his face, and he put his hands on either side of my face, "Oh God, did someone hurt you, Child?" he said.

Child? Why did my stomach tighten when he said that?

"Only my pride," I answered, ashamed to be on the verge of tears.

Wilkins left my side long enough to pour me a glass of port. Then he covered me with a thick blanket. He set an equally thick blanket down beside my chair, and knelt in front of me to remove my shoes.

"Here, what are you doing?"

"Would you rather lose a toe?" answered my new host firmly, "Rubbing the feet gets the blood circulating. Get that port down your gullet, there's a good girl."

I had forgotten how exacting he was when taking care of someone. Thirsty and desperate for my first taste of liquor in months, I obeyed. The blood-colored wine glided down my throat as honey down a spoon. I closed my eyes and let the flavor take me. I heard him walk away into another room. In a few moments, his footsteps returned to me. The silk of his banyan hissed as he knelt down before me.

"Ruby, open your eyes," he said. He was holding a red clay bowl, which was a quarter of the way full of soup. He carefully removed the glass from my hands and replaced it with the warm bowl. The soup smelled heavenly, and I could finally being to feel my hands resurrecting themselves.

"My first year at sea was spent in the galley," said Joe with a wink. "That old sea-cook taught me well. I added a bit of cold water, so you can take it now. Drink up, Puss."

I sipped the hot liquid. It was the best soup I had ever tasted.

"You can cook, clean, mend and deliver babies, Joe. You will make an excellent wife one day."

Joe laughed and kissed my forehead. He drew closer and adjusted the blankets around me, rubbing my shoulders and arms. He was so close I could smell the soap he used. I could feel the gentle strength in his hands. I didn't want him to stop rubbing. I wanted him to rub me everywhere. I was quivering in my petticoats before this handsome, kind man. A seafaring man. A man's man. A deliciously wonderful man.

Stop thinking about all that and drink the damn soup!

"What happened, Ruby?" he said as he covered my legs and feet with the remaining blanket and took his own chair.

"Don't want to talk about it, thank you, Doc," I answered quietly as I stared into the empty bowl in my hands. "Look," I finally said, "could I just stay here for just a few days? I have nowhere else to go."

"Here?" he asked, "But I thought you were at Urania Cottage?"

"I won't be missed all that much, I'm sure."

"Ruby, what happ—"

"Please, don't ask me anymore," I pleaded, my eyelids fit to collapse, "Please."

Wilkins stroked my hair. My stomach tightened again at his touch. I shivered. *I'm still chilled. Yes, that must be it.*

The fire, the port and soup were doing their jobs well, and I began to nod off.

"Very well. But tomorrow I'll need to —"

"I just want to sleep," I heard myself interrupt him. "Please."

I felt Wilkins lift me into his arms. "I'm putting you to bed, Ruby," he whispered softly, "good thing I already passed the warming pan through the sheets." He put me down on something soft and put his hands on my middle. I struggled a bit, and he whispered to me again, "Don't be afraid. You'll sleep easier without the corset."

Even through the corset, I could feel his hands on me. I laid my head on his shoulder and let him undo the laces.

"Stay," I heard myself whisper.

"Naughty puss," chuckled Joe as he discarded my corset, "You don't owe me anything."

"I know," I whispered back, and nuzzled into his neck.

"You don't know what you're saying, Ruby. You're exhausted."

"But I—"

"Hush, girl. You're safe. Sleep as long as you like."

I sighed and gave in to my fatigue. I felt him guide my head gently down onto the pillow, and draw the warm sheets and blankets up to my chin.

I never even heard the door close as he left the room.

CHAPTER XIX

OF FRIENDS, CHEESE, BOOKS...AND THINGS BEST LEFT HIDDEN.

"This Cottage business is consuming you, my dear Charles," said Forster as we sat at The George in Southwark. Seated within in the Parliament Bar, I now enjoyed a drink my truest friend.

"It's all worth it, Forster," I responded, "Even to save just one. And each one of them a fascinating study."

"I've no doubt, Charles. But are you sure you are not too taken with this Lilac, or Ruby, or whatever her name is?"

"*Taken* by her?" I asked in as seemingly an unaffected manner as I could muster, "Odd choice of words, Forster." I had not told him about that night with Ruby in my study.

"She is a charming girl to be sure, Charles. Full of fire. And her uncanny resembl-"

"Has nothing to do with anything!" I hurriedly snapped. Forster flashed those wonderful, terrible, stern eyes at me, and waited.

"Forgive me," said I, "I just don't want you getting the wrong idea. Her - appearance - is immaterial to the story."

"As you say, Charles," returned my friend graciously, as he sipped his madeira.

"I *do* say," I added quickly. "Anyway, what were we talking of before?"

"Where to dine this evening."

"Ah yes. Well, in any case, I should like to remain here a while longer. The atmosphere is inspiring to me. Do you mind, Forster?"

"So long as we eat, I shall be content," answered Forster with a pat of his waistcoat.

"Thank you, my friend. Now," I said as I poured us both more Madeira, "shall we have another glass? Another bottle? Yes. It is on me, as is supper." I said the last of this loud enough for the barkeep to hear. He looked over and nodded in acknowledgement.

"You are too good, Charles," said Forster with a smile.

"Yes, well don't advertise it, please."

Forster began to chuckle, mid gulp, which (aided by the bottle we had already consumed) made me chuckle.

"If I may," said Forster into his sleeve as he wiped his mouth with it, "return to our other topic if but for a moment, I must congratulate you on your choice of books for Urania. However, I was surprised to find you had included none of your own. At the very least, I think you should add *A Christmas Carol* as well as *Oliver Twist*."

"Really? You don't think it too vain?"

"Vain? Ha! From the mouth of the man who sits right under Dr Johnson's portrait at The Cheese! Ha, vain, indeed!" He laughed hard at this.

"Correction, sits to the right under the portrait," I chuckled. "Hm, cheese. Ha, Walter was looking at a picture book the other day. Cheese was one of the words he had the most trouble with. You should have heard him, 'Ch - ch - eee- eee - eeeeee - thhhh!' Oh, John, it was hilarious!"

Forster laughed. "Didn't you say once that you learned to read above a cheese monger's, Charles?"

"Mmm," I uttered as I finished another glass. "I remember the books very well. They smelled of soap. Remarkable, actually, considering that everything from Dodd's Grocery in the corner opposite usually smelled of streaky bacon."

"And that was where, again?" mumbled Forster to no one in particular as he retrieved the notebook from his coat pocket. "Oh yes," he said as he found the notation, "Um," he looked about to make sure we were alone before continuing to address me in the most quiet of whispers, "Norfolk Street, was it? Near that Workhouse? Do you remember mentioning it? You lived there twice, um, before and, um, after-"

The wine caught in my throat as if I had swallowed an angry bee. *Damn, why did I ever tell you? I brought us here because I thought I was ready. I thought forcing myself to be so close to the place of Father's shame (within walking distance of us at this very moment!) would produce the long needed exorcism. But I just cannot talk about it, Forster, not yet. I know why you are pressing me, but I will not budge.* I managed to gulp down the wine with only a slight cough. My left hand began to tremble, and I lowered it under the table and clenched my thigh.

"Charles, are you well?" inquired my friend.

"Never mind it, Forster," I replied as plainly as I could.

Dickens and the Whore

"Come, now. You know you may confide in me."

"Oh, Forster," I sighed as I leaned back and looked up at the ceiling, "must we go through this again? What does it matter where I lived as a boy? What does any of it matter? I know you have designs on my life story, but none of that will be of the slightest interest to anyone, I assure you. It's the stories I create that they thrive upon, not my own."

"On the contrary, my friend," returned Forster, "they love you."

"Well then, my Boswell," I said, "this loved one requests his privacy. I mean how would you feel to have your childhood traced in every way? It's absurd."

"Then why have you shared that unfortunate time with me, Charles?"

"Because you are the truest friend I have or have ever had, and I had to tell someone..."

In the ensuing moments, I heard all Forster said, but could not answer. Recollections were taking over, and this time their hold was too strong. I began to fidget. Nay, I trembled. It went all up my back, up and down the left side of my body. Lightning struck from within. The flame of the candle on the table became as the light of a train in a long dark tunnel, searching for a way out. *A way out...the dark...of...the black...Blacking...Warren's Blacking...*

I seized the empty bottle and began to peel and pick at the label frantically. *Pasting labels, sealing pots, pasting labels, sealing pots...No, I don't want to remember!*

But it was no use. The bottle changed. It became a tan, clay pot, whose plain, disgusting design was abhorrent to behold. The table became bare and foul. The thick odor of the blacking was suddenly under my nose, along with the stench of rats and sweat of street boys, the heat and the grime covered me once again.

A way out...I have to get out!

I looked up, but Forster was no longer in my vision. The factory window I had slaved in front of for twelve grueling, miserable, nightmarish months was before me. I glanced back down at my hands, which were now the cramped, squalid hands of my twelve year old self.

Father, for God's sake get me out! This place is like a prison. Prison. No, you are in a prison. It's your fault. You can't even get yourself out...out of debt...out of prison...the one word that was as plague to my brain...MARSHALSEA!!!

"...And I am proud to be your friend, Charles," continued Forster. "And as your friend, let me say that growing up in the shadow of a Workhouse will only add to the mystique of the man who penned *Twist*. Why, the public-"

NO! *No one must know. No one must EVER know! Oh, Father, I love you. But how could you? The son of servants reduced to a debtor's prison. Sending me to Warren's - an entire year in that hellish factory! Abandoning your child to Purgatory on The Strand; you don't know what that did to me! The secret agony; the shame I can never voice, save through my characters. But for Grandmother's death, I would have BECOME The*

Artful Dodger. Aye, Forster, you'd like to know all about that too, wouldn't you - you would have the world know how the inheritance she left paid my Father's debts? AND I HAVE PAID THEM EVER SINCE! Death and money, death and money...Confound this family of mine! Dickenses - Devils, Aye! Devils All! Must I hold us all up alone forever? FATHER!

Suddenly, I was back. The table was as it had been. I was no longer holding a bottle of blacking, but an empty bottle of Madeira. I tossed it as if it were the wrong end of a hot poker. It fell onto the table and rolled, taking itself and the candlestick to the floor with a ferocious clang.

"DAMN THE PUBLIC!" I hissed as leaned in and shot him a glance fit to frighten Beelzebub. "Do I not have a say in the dealings of my own life? Or must I unpack my heart before all the world because my name is a household word? No, by God. And no, again!" I buried my head in my hands and tried to control my breathing.

"Calm down, my dear fellow," whispered my patient friend as he leaned in. "Calm down. Thank God this place is empty at this time of day..."

"Forster," I said, my head still down and my voice dry and harsh, "I implore you, as my friend. Do not print this. If the public wish to understand me, my published works will supply all they need know." I looked up, "In the name of God, will that not suffice?"

"Very well, Charles," said my friend kindly, "Of course. Now calm yourself-"

"Swear!" I said, fighting back tears as I gripped his wrist, "Swear you will never print any of it. Please, if you love me, Friend-"

Forster placed his other hand over mine, "Charles, my word on it, Friend. I so swear."

"Thank you, John," I sighed. Just then, the barman returned with clean glasses, warm bread, and another bottle of Madeira. He started a bit when he saw the candlestick and broken bottle upon the floor.

"Everything alright, Gentlemen? You ain't been disturbed, have you?"

"No. Um, yes, um, yes, thank you. Just acting out a scene to make sure I get the details right. So sorry for the trouble."

"It must be a right tosser. I look forward to reading it, Sir! Be back with a broom to tidy this up for you in a tiff."

I smiled at him as he took his leave of us again. *I shall have to tip him well.* Forster quickly poured my glass and helped my hand to it.

"A toast," I said as my voice cracked with emotion, "to true friendship."

"To 'The Inimitable'," said Forster with a wink as he filled his glass.

"And to his secrets," I concluded, as our glasses clinked.

CHAPTER XX

RUBY LEARNS THE NATURE OF TRUE LOVE.

I spent five blissful days under his roof. Joe gave me a rose-coloured cotton dress—the family or a former patient had requested they go to a good cause. He braved the cold to procure stockings, shawl, gloves and a bonnet. I fought back the outburst to throw my arms around him, but did kiss his cheek. So help me, he blushed!

The weather had been very cold, and we had spent the past few nights by the fire in my (well, Joe's) bedroom. He would make the cheese on toast and I the drinking chocolate. We sat on blankets and surrounded ourselves with toe warmers full of coals to heat the space. We talked of many things. Joe regaled me with the first time he saw a sperm whale up close off the coast of some far off place called Peru. It could take a year just to get to this strange place! And he told me of the people of the Sandwich Islands, the beauty of the women, and the exotic, beautiful flowers there. At half past ten every night, Joe took his leave of me and retired to the parlour. I offered to trade rooms with him several times, but he insisted that I sleep in the bed.

I agreed to keep the place tidy while he made his daily patient rounds, which also often included the nearby Workhouse in Union Street, or back at Tothill Fields. Though an adjoining room off of his parlour housed his surgery, no patients called. Joe explained to me that he would often close his surgery until the weather became warmer, or some desperate soul knocked at his door.

"If someone is ill," he said, "venturing out in this chilly air could do them harm. It is better for me to go to them."

And so our routine continued for a week. Then, over breakfast the next day, Joe began to press me for more information about why I had come to him.

"Ruby, I am delighted to have you stay here. But it isn't proper."

"But no one needs to know I'm here," I said, sounding a bit more like a whining child than I cared to. I took another bite of toast to stifle myself.

"Live here like some stowaway? Never venturing out? No, Ruby. I won't have it."

"Fine," I said, rising from my chair. I walked to his front door.

"Stop!" he barked.

"What do you care?" I barked back. "You don't want me."

He grabbed me by the arms.

"You have no idea what I want. Think, you foolish girl. Where will you go? You have no money, no other clothes."

"I'll earn them. I've done it before."

"Ruby, for God's sake why won't you talk to me? Don't you trust me?"

"I am not going back to Urania," I answered vehemently, adding a stomp of my foot.

Joe stepped away from me, and hung his head. Then he looked up at me and crossed his arms.

"So you are just going to give up? I was wrong about you, then. You really are a selfish bitch."

His words hit me as if he had struck me. I began to cry like a little girl.

"Joe," I whimpered. I took a step toward him, but he turned and walked away. *I want to tell you, Joe. I want to tell you everything. It's just that I'm so afraid! Please, if you thought ill of me, I couldn't bear it.*

"Never a thought to what anyone else goes through, so long as you get what you want. Fine, stay here then. I could never make you leave. You can have your way. You always do."

He entered his surgery. The door slammed behind him. I jumped at the sound, and began to cry harder. His cruel words had made me feel so small. I sat before the fire, and tried to control my sobs. I lifted my head to take a few deep breaths, and noticed something on the mantel. Two opened letters. *Those weren't there when I cleaned yesterday.* I rose and picked them up. The letters were from Edinburgh, and address to Joe. The hand was delicate; feminine. I sat back down near the fire and read the first one.

My Dearest Joe,
Mother shall not last much longer. Her lungs are weak, as you know. She begged me not to tell you, to spare you the journey. "There is nothing he can do for me," she said. "My boy is better off tending the living." But I write to you for my own sake, my dearest Joe. Please come home. It has been so tiresome without you. I am lonely.
~Grace.

The other letter was written the day I had arrived.

My Dearest Joe,
Mother breathed her last yesterday. Her last words were of you, my dear. My heart is too heavy to tell you more. Please come home to me, Dear Joe.
~Grace.

Dear Joe? Is she his wife? Shit. He was too good to be true.

I fought back tears of rage as I carefully put the letter back in its envelope.

Why did I ever trust him? He just wants me like…hell, like every other man I've ever known!

But this man saved my life. He took me in.

Aye, so he did. And so did Top. You forget how that turned out?

No, I haven't forgotten. But Joe is different.

Prove it, clever puss.

I shall!

I walked to the surgery door and knocked.

"Go away," hollered Joe. His voice was strained. *My God, is he crying?*

"If you didn't want to be disturbed, you should have bolted it," I said as I entered. Joe was seated in his chair, elbows on the desk, his head between his hands. He had no banyan over his shirt, and there was no fire in the grate. The lamp on the table was nearly out of whale oil, its two tiny wicks choking at their own diligence to duty.

"It's cold in here," I said, "Come back in the drawing room with me."

"Parlour."

"Whatever. You'll get ill if you stay in here."

He just snorted. There was a bottle of whiskey and a full glass next to him. He reached out for the glass, but I covered the opening with my palm.

"I'm sorry, Joe."

Joe sighed, "You're young, Ruby. It's fine."

"No it isn't," I insisted quietly, "Your Ma—"

His head shot up.

"I—I read the letter. I know I shouldn't have, but I wanted to know—"

"It's fine, Ruby," he simply said again.

"Stop saying that, Joe," I said, moving closer. "You knew she was dying and you stayed."

"My mother was dying. I couldn't have saved her," he answered, "that made you the priority."

"But she was your mother. Didn't you love her?"

"Very much," he answered. His voice was barely a whisper.

"Then why didn't you—"

The look in his brown eyes gave me the answer. My heart began to race, and I fought to not cry again.

"Ruby," said Joe as he took both my hands in his. I slipped one hand out of his and touched his cheek.

"Hush," I ordered as he let me pull him to his feet, "I am putting you to bed."

"I'm not tired."

"Come along, Boots."

Joe practically passed out as his head hit the pillow. I removed his slippers, covered him with the blankets, blew out the lamps, and got in to the opposite side of the bed. I looked over at him.

Enough light from the fire allowed me to notice his cheeks were still wet. I reached out my hand and gently wiped them away.

"Sister," whispered Joe. His words carried the faintest hint of whiskey.

"What?"

"The letters are from my sister."

I let go a breath I didn't know I had held, and kissed his forehead. I felt at peace touching him, being next to him like this. Then I listened for a while to the sound of his breathing, and finally fell asleep.

I slept as I never had before. I awoke to find I had turned in the night, and was now facing Joe. His arm was still around my waist, and I moved closer to him. I looked at his face. The strong jaw, the cheeks. The graceful arch of his dark auburn eyebrows. This man was good looking. This man was kind. This man saved my life, gave me shelter, fed me and demanded nothing in return. This man put me above his dying mother. This man was willing to let me go again to finish my time at Urania. This man wanted me, but only on my terms. This man loved me. Me. And I hadn't done a goddamned thing to get him.

I kissed Joe's lips. He smiled and giggled deeply in his sleep, and his hold on me tightened. As he unconsciously pulled me closer, I put my head against his broad, warm chest, and closed my eyes.

Had I had known falling in the Thames would hasten the day I met my true love, I would have plunged into its filthy maw ages ago.

CHAPTER XXI

A DREADFUL MISTAKE.

I awoke to find Joe gone. He had left a note on his pillow.

> My Darling Miss Puss,
> Thank you. You would make a very fine nurse. I have gone to Union Street Workhouse this evening. Will return late, as I left late. Waking in the arms of a beautiful Faerie makes leaving the bed a loathsome task. Joe.

My heart fluttered as I giggled and kissed his missive. Then I rose and washed my face, and threw my shawl about my shoulders. The parlour was still warm; Joe had not been gone long. He had cleared away our breakfast, too. I walked to the cabinet opposite the fire and looked for what we would read together tonight. The clock struck half-past eight. *We slept through the entire day!*

A basket of knitted goods for the Workhouse was still in his chair. *Joe must have forgotten it.*

It had been nearly a week since I had been outside, and I saw no harm in hailing a cab and dropping the basket outside the gate. *I won't leave the carriage. I'll just have the driver ring the bell and lay the basket by the gate. It will take ten minutes at most!* I fixed my hair, put on my bonnet and shawl, and went down to hail a cab. One stopped and I shouted up the address to the driver as

I got in. The cab made its way out of Burton Crescent and onto Marchmont, then turned right and travelled down along Tavistock.

But then, instead of going straight down the road to make the turn to Union Street, the cab turned right, into a small side street. In the lamplight, I could make out a street sign that read, Charlotte Mews.

The horse stopped. But for the lamps on the cab, all was still and dark within the Mews. Something was very wrong, and I own that my heart began to pound.

"Driver," I said as I tapped on the roof of the cab, "What the hell do you think—?"

The sound of a match striking startled me. It was quickly followed by the high pitched creek of the little door above my head as it opened. The lamp shone down through the hole bright as sunlight, blinding me from seeing its keeper. The voice I heard was one I knew well.

> Ah! heedless girl! why thus disclose
> What ne'er was meant for other ears;
> Why thus destroy thine own repose
> And dig the source of future tears?

I drew in a ragged breath. The doors of the cab suddenly flew open, and I screamed.

"Top?" I called softly. The cab moved as the driver leapt down. I heard boots on the cobbles to my left. Their pace was deliberate; they bid me wait to behold whatever was coming for me. But I had no intention of waiting. I flew out of the cab on the right side and ran back to the entrance of the Mews. The footsteps were soon upon me, and I was seized by the arm, a hand over my mouth. I knew those arms. They spun me around.

"Top!" I cried, "What are you doing?"

"Did I not tell you never to leave me?"

"I was attacked. I fell into the Thames."

"That was months ago! I know where you have been since, and I have waited until the right moment—"

"Top, I wanted to contact you, but they would not let me."

"Since when does Ruby Waller follow anyone's rules but her own?" barked Top. "You think me an idiot? Think I didn't know where you went those nights? Keeping company with famous Dandy's and handsome doctors, eh? You would cast me off that easily, the man who saved your wretched little life!"

"So I should come back with you and be your plaything again?"

"I loved you! I never hurt you!" Top roared, heartbroken.

"Not in body, Top," I answered, my head held high, "but in soul, you killed me."

Top drew a knife from his belt, a look of complete madness in his eyes.

"And now I shall finish the job."

His other hand came over mine. There was a foul smell on the handkerchief that made me dizzy. I held my breath and wriggled and kicked to try to free myself, but his grip only tightened. He pulled me toward the lamp he had set down on the cobbles.

I decided to feign drowsiness in the hope that he would release me. I let my body grow limp and soon the handkerchief had vanished and he was lowering me to the ground. I could feel the heat of the lamp near my head as Top continued his recitation of Byron as he ripped open my bodice.

> Oh, thou wilt weep, imprudent maid,
> While lurking envious foes will smile,
> "For all the follies thou has said
> Of those who spoke but to beguile.

I felt the knife on my collarbone, and tried to hold my breath steady.

"Top!" someone called. He looked up. I knew that voice, too. It was the man who had saved me from the Thames, the one who had warned me to leave Urania.

"Ah, Matthew. It has been too long, little brother," said Top.

Little brother? Of course, the green eyes! Suddenly I was no longer certain if my inability to catch my breath was due to Top's knife or the revelation unfolding before me.

"You were always more concerned with appearances than I," said the voice again.

"Step this way, Matthew," said Top, "lest I let my knife slip."

Matthew obeyed. "Ruby?" he said as he walked.

"Matthew," I whispered.

"The sea has aged you a bit," Top observed.

"It's all up, brother," said Matthew.

"Indeed, I am certain you did not come alone." said Top as he grinned. "Mr. Dickens, this is an unexpected pleasure. Step forward if you please, Sir."

Dandy appeared from the shadows, a lantern in one hand, a pistol in the other. His gaze was as hot as the flame he held.

"Release her," he said. His voice was as low as I had ever heard it. In that moment, I believed him capable of pulling the trigger.

"She's mine," Top growled, "You sought to take my angel from me—the only woman I ever loved!"

"You do not love," sneered Dickens, disgusted.

Top's knife pressed closer on my skin, "Tell them, my love. Tell them I never hurt you, how I cared for you and tended you. Tell them!"

Dickens looked at me as if to say: *Keep him calm. Say what he wants to hear.*

"What you say is true, Top. You did take me in. I had been raped, and you tended my wounds. You kissed away my tears and let me sleep in a warm, soft bed. You let me live with you. When I was well, you gave me dresses and dolls. Aye, you took good care of me, I couldn't have asked for more. And I fell in love with you, but was too shy to say it. When I came of age, you told me you loved me. That was the first night we made love. Remember?"

"I was gentle as I could be," Top said, his voice trembling with emotion.

"Always," I answered, my hands creeping up to touch his face. His eyes closed at my touch, and he shuddered.

"Why did you leave me?" he strained, hoarse with emotion.

"Because I was frightened. You were true to me, Top. You were all I knew. Yes, I left you, and now you mean to kill me. I want to meet my maker with a clean conscience. Don't you see? I was never worthy of you, my darling. You were always kind with me; you deserved much more than a little street cat like me. I hurt you, and I am sorry—"

"Enough!" he shouted. *If he pushes any harder on that knife, I'm out of print!*

I thought of Joe, and imagined his reaction to my bloodless corpse.

No! I will not die like this. Keep your voice steady and sweet. Make Top think you mean it, or it's your life!

"Top, if you love me, let me live. Let me make amends. Come away with me to Australia. I am supposed to go there next year, but I don't want to wait now that we're together again. Dickens will pay for it, won't you?"

"Indeed, yes," he answered, and lowered his pistol as he added, "Ruby has chosen you, Sir. I can arrange passage on a ship as soon as tomorrow." *You are a good actor, Dandy!*

"And we can have a new life," I added, "away from Maters, Mousies and meddlers. Just you and me!"

The blade left my neck.

"Ruby," whispered Top. He voice was as reverent as if he had beheld Christ's mother.

"Come away with me, Top," I whispered back.

"You lying bastard."

I could smell her before I heard her voice. We all looked into the darkened mews as Mousie emerged. Her ugly face was twisted into fury. Top laughed.

"Too stupid to know I was using you to find Ruby! You never were good for anything, my child."

"Nor was you. Pa."

"Pa?" I cried.

"I should never have lived," said Mousie as she drew a small pistol from her cream apron.

Top's knife sped like a dart to her chest, and she fell. I kicked him hard in the crotch. My hands were still on his face. The image of Collette's pathetic, lifeless eyes came to me and in anger I began to slap him. He paused, shattered that I had raised a hand to him. His lip actually began to tremble. The rage of seven years deception overtook me at last, and thrust my thumbs into his eyes. It felt like grapes bursting; their contents poured down my fingers, onto my face and into my mouth. He shrieked over and over, and rolled to one side. I seized the pistol and threw it into the darkness, then scrambled to my feet. Matthew and Dickens were already at my side.

A gargling noise and the click of metal caused Matthew to whirl around. Two shots rang out, almost simultaneously, and Top's cries suddenly ceased. My left shoulder went very hot, as if a branding iron had been plunged to the very bone. Dickens caught me as the world faded.

"Ruby! Oh God, please no."

CHAPTER XXII

TO THE STRAND UNION WORKHOUSE—AND THE TRUTH WILL OUT!

"Go!" Matthew shouted, "I'll take matters in hand here. Wilkins is at Strand Union Workhouse."

He managed to stop the horse (and subsequently the cab) from bolting at the sound of the pistol shots and trampling us all. I lifted Ruby into the cab and leapt up to the driver's seat.

"I'll take her to him," I declared as I slapped the reigns. That horse ran like hell fire down Goodge Street then Cleveland Street, arriving at the Workhouse. I jumped to the street and got Ruby out of the cab.

"Open the gate! I need a doctor urgently. Open the gate!"

An old man dashed out and obliged. He paled when he saw the blood, and gave me leave to enter quickly.

"Fetch two litters and make for the Charlotte Mews, immediately!" I roared as I entered. The old man, his step a bit more brisk, shuffled over to take my instructions.

"Use the cab outside. Find two more strong men and make haste," I ordered, "I will pay handsomely for speed."

"As you wish. Doctor's on the top floor, Sir!" said the old man.

I ran up those stairs in what seemed but half a second.

"Wilkins!" I shouted, "Where are you, man?"

"Dickens?" cried Joe, who quickly emerged from a room, drying his hands with a towel. "What the dev—Ruby! Jesus Christ!" He took her from me and carried to the room across the hall. There were three empty beds on either side. We laid Ruby on the bed closest to the fire grate.

"She's been shot in the shoulder," I said. *It's the left shoulder, just like Oliver Twist.*

"I can see that!" said an exasperated Wilkins. "Now get out. I won't have the likes of you underfoot. Wait below."

I looked down at my hands. They were trembling and bloodstained. Her blood.

"I -"

"Get out, Dickens!" bellowed Wilkins as he carefully cut up the length of her sleeve.

I turned and exited back into the passage. Half way down the steps, the two men who had helped carry Ruby up were bearing another load. It was Matthew. He was clasping his side.

"Mousie weren't quite dead," he said in a strained voice. "Yet. Had more pistols on her."

"Wilkins!" I shouted as I darted back up to him, "Your patient load has just increased, I'm afraid."

We deposited Matthew on the bed next to Ruby.

"You've been Shanghaied, Boz," said Wilkins, his eyes never leaving his work, "Keep pressure on his side. I almost have the bullet out of her arm."

I did as instructed. "Stay with us, Matthew. There's a good fellow."

"Good, Dickens. Keep jawing with him, even if he doesn't answer. Don't stop."

Matthew opened his eyes. "The truth," he said. The sound of the bullet clanked into a tin tray, I sent silent thanks to the Almighty.

"Save your strength, shipmate," said Wilkins to Matthew as he threaded a needle.

I began to rub Matthew's temples in order to help calm him - a useful tool in Mesmerism which had served me well many times before. "The doctor is right. Besides, did you think the fact the similarity of your eyes to Top's would escape my notice?"

"No," said Matthew, "just didn't want it to be about me. My aim was to help Ruby, and that's all."

"I understand," I answered softly.

"Top?" asked Wilkins, "Where is that flaming bastard?"

"By now, I would say below waiting for a Workhouse funeral," said I.

"Ruby put his lights out," said Matthew, "and I finished him off. Him and his tainted offspring."

"You know Ruby?" inquired Wilkins, "Hold still now," he continued as he assessed the wound.

"Aye," answered Matthew, who kept still. His eyes looked straight at the ceiling. "Mousie were Top's child," he swallowed hard.

"By whom?" I asked.

"By our own mother, Collette."

"Jesus Christ," said Wilkins, "some family you've got, Lad."

Matthew winced again, but I knew not if it was from his wound or the memory. "Top went mad years ago. Father died penniless, and our mother took it hard. Then she took it out on us. More so on Top. Though he were older, he was sickly and weak. One day during a thrashing, he rose up and beat her instead. Before I knew it, he was raping her. She begged me to stop him, but I—That was the day I left."

"How is it you chose this time to return?" I asked.

"Mother got a letter to me. Somehow, he never found out. Made it all the way to the Sandwich Islands on a whale ship, then to me at one of them Reading Rooms for Sailors. She begged me to return. I never replied. God forgive me."

He coughed. By now, Wilkins had removed the young man's shirt and was ready to close the wound. "That's enough now. You're lucky Mousie's aim was so bad; the knife passed through flesh only. Best to stitch you up. I'll be as quick as I can, Shipmate."

"You're a seafaring man, Doc?" asked Matthew.

"Aye," said Joe, "when I was a young pup like you. Better put this between your teeth."

The doctor placed a small, long dented strap of dark leather in Matthew's mouth, then turned to me. "Dickens, have you a flask?"

I nodded and administered some brandy to the patient.

"There's a good lad," said Wilkins. "Now Dickens, hold him still."

CHAPTER XXIII

RUBY DREAMS OF HER TRAGIC FALL.

We had just exited the Church of Saint Martin-in-the-Fields, when Mr. Banning continued his explanation as to why we had journeyed there. I had thought it a nice service and I had never been to a church that big before.

The whole area smelled of horse shit and foods of all sorts being cooked.

"Thank you for letting me light a candle for my parents," I said.

"Your Pa and Ma are gone, Ruby," said Banning as we stood a few paces away from the doors, "Ain't my fault your mother was weak. And I ain't gonna be the left one to raise you. Girls are expensive."

"But where shall I live?" I asked, frightened.

We stopped and he took out his pocket watch. Then he looked intently at the crowds. Seeing a man at the far right of the church steps, leaning against a large column, he smiled.

"With him."

He held onto my hand and led me to the stranger. He was very large, and not very clean. His brown coat and what had once been cream trousers were neither clean nor pressed. His cheek was protruding to one side, and he moved his jaw as if he were chewing something. No one spoke, but we all continued to walk down the side steps and up the street a while. We stopped at the opening of a long and very narrow passage to our right.

"This man is your new Pa," Banning said to me. "Mind him."

I gasped, "What?"

"Is she fresh?" asked the strange man. He turned his head and spit out a mass of brown, foul smelling juice.

Banning smiled, "As fresh as morning dew drops. Kept her that way just for you."

The man looked at me and smiled. His teeth were oozing with the same color as the tobacco he had spit.

"Good. Not like the last one you sold me, then. Pity that boy didn't work out. I'm partial to his sort."

"She'll make up for it, never you fear."

I may have only been ten years old, but I knew something was very wrong.

"Please, don't make me go with him," I said to Mr. Banning. "If I've done something wrong, I'll make it right. I won't be a bother, I promise!"

But the stranger thrust a purse of coins at Banning, and in turn he pushed me into the other man's arms. He held me tight and looked down at me hungrily. He smiled, and I felt as if I would retch at the sight of his stained, rotten teeth.

"Come along, my little pretty."

"No! I don't want to!"

The man slapped me hard and I yelped. Anger I had never felt reared up, and I bit down on his hand as hard as I could. He cried out and stepped back.

The large man pinned Banning to the wall and took back his coin purse.

"You said this one would mind! To hell with you, Banning. I'll find what I need in Seven Dials. No lack of tight young pussy there."

Then he stomped off, swearing. Banning's hands crushed my small arms, and he shook me like a paper doll.

"You little bitch! You just cost me good money!"

He dragged me into an alley that was so tight he had to drag me behind him. We walked about twenty paces before instinct took over. I bit down on his hand as hard as I could. He cried out and released me. I ran back toward the street, but he caught me and carried me back into the alley, his hand over my mouth. After walking a few more paces that we had reached originally, he put me down and turned me to face him.

"Quiet! Or I'll take you up this street and sell your little ass to a brothel in Seven Dials, where the likes of him can fuck you. That what you want, girl?"

"Wha—What's a bro—brothel?" I asked in gulps.

"It's where they do this."

He picked me up and slammed my back to the brick. My legs were astride him. His hand reached up my petticoat. Then he unbuttoned his trousers and jammed himself inside me. The pain was so great I could not breathe. I could not scream. I could not move. I could not think. Banning grunted and moaned as he took his full fill, ramming my back over and over against the brick wall. With each thrust, I felt as if I were being torn apart.

He gave one final grunt, and looked at me as I slid to the ground. I sat in my own blood.

"And it's all you'll ever be good for," he panted.

He tossed two coins at my feet, and walked away.

"Easiest bit of coin you'll ever earn, little whore."

I lay there on the cobbles, unable to think. I watched my hand reach out and grasp the coins. I do not know how much time passed. But, at length, a stained apron came into my vision. I heard someone speak to me.

"What you crying for, then?"

I looked up. The apron gave way to a light blue (and very dirty) dress. It was a young girl, about my age, but smaller. From under a red bonnet, her freckled face and bucked teeth beheld me with contempt. Her long, dark brown hair hung straight as a sheet around her, as did her skirt, devoid of petticoats but one, from which a foul smell was coming. She stunk like rancid cheese and dead fish.

"He hurt me," I whimpered.

"Be glad it's over," the girl snapped back. "Besides, you've stopped bleeding."

"Please, help me. Call a policeman."

"Don't you know where you are?"

"No," I sniffed.

"Brydge's Place. Porridge Island."

I stood and took a step. I fell over again in pain.

"I can't—"

"Follow me or stay here and starve," said the smaller girl, devoid of any feeling as she turned and walked on, "it ain't no never mind to me."

She was right, it wasn't far. She led me through the long alleyway to the door of a house a few streets from the passage. A grey haired woman with pinched features opened it and peered out.

"Who's she?" asked the woman, inclining her head in my direction.

"Found her. Thought she may be of use."

Mousie led me through the front hall to a large room on the left.

"Sit down," the woman said.

"I can't," I said timidly.

"Why can't you? The sofa not grand enough for your highness?"

"Please—" I said as she backed me to the wall, "I'm hurt."

"Are you refusing my hospitality?"

"No, but I—"

Her bony hand landed across my cheek and sent me to the carpet. The coins, still clutched in my hand, darted across the room to the feet of a man who now stood leaning against the parlour door. Lean and tall, he eyed me with a confidence and sharpness I had never seen. He wore a Robin's egg blue coat with dark blue velvet trim over a waistcoat of brown silk. His riding trousers were tan, his black boots came up to his knees. He still held a riding crop in his hand, which he tapped against his thigh as he addressed my attacker. His bright, green eyes were set upon me. He was the most handsome, dashing, well-dressed Gentleman I had ever seen.

"Come now, Mater, dear. Is that any way to treat a helpless child? And such a pretty little thing, too." His tone was lofty, and I could tell he was angry at her for hurting me. It gave me hope that perhaps following the smelly girl was the right thing to do.

"Top," said the old woman, her face stretched in panic, "Didn't expect you so soon."

"Business finished early," he said as he approached me, "Made an excellent take tonight. Well, my, where did they find you, little lamb?"

"Brydge's Place. Crying her blasted eyes out." answered Mousie.

He reached out to pick me up, and I cowered and hid my face under my arm and began to cry.

"Hush now," he soothed as he ran his hand over the top of my head. "I see the dried blood, you poor child. Just happened, has it? You need a soft warm bed and a nip for the pain. Come now, Top will see that you get everything you need. Be a good girl. Trust me."

His voice. The sincerity and softness with which he spoke to me! I nodded my head, and he lifted me into his arms. He was warm and he smelled of sweet tobacco and soft hay.

"Mousie," said Top as he stood, "fetch warm water, towels, ointment and the vinegar bottle. Now."

She did not hesitate, and began the task of fetching and preparing the things he requested with all speed. Top walked to the parlour door and turned to face Mater, who still had not moved.

"I'll deal with you later, Madam," he said coldly. Then he looked down at me as he walked through the small foyer to the stairs.

"They always do what I say, you know. Always. They won't be harsh with you anymore." Then he gave the tip of my nose a gentle, playful peck with his lips. I managed a small smile, and nuzzled my head in his neck.

The chamber was large, with a fire on the far wall and a great, magnificent window, framed by faded crimson drapes. He laid me tenderly down on the bed, and began to undress me. I screamed and tried to fend him off. Mousie entered just then with a large pan and a bottle.

"Stop that, child," he said gently. "Didn't I promise not to hurt you? You need to be washed off. The vinegar may sting going in, but it will be worth it, and the ointment will sooth the pain after, I promise."

It did sting. A great bloody lot. Top held me steady as I screamed, reassuring me that I would be alright. Mousie then left the chamber, unmoved by the sight of my injuries and pain.

"I'm sorry Mater struck you," said Top as he tucked me in. "She sometimes thinks she can treat children like dogs. But she is the dog, and like a dog, must be reminded of her place. She will be punished for what she did."

He removed the coins from his pocket. "Here, my lamb. These belong to you," he said as he held them out to me.

"I don't want them!" I said as I sobbed and turned my head away.

"Do they frighten you?" asked Top.

"Yes!" I cried.

"Top will help you conquer your fears," he said. He walked to the mantle and reached behind a shelf on the left hand side. As if by magic, he produced an old Twinings tin. "This will be your box, little one. Forgive me. I don't know your name, my sweet. What is it?"

"It's R—Ruby," I said, my sniffs subsiding at long last.

"Ruby," he said with a bow, "this is Ruby's box," continued Top, holding the box up as if it were the Crown Jewels, "Her secret box, that only she and her Top knows about." Then he replaced the box in its hiding place, and winked. The laudanum was taking its toll on me. The last thing I remember is the brush of his lips on my forehead as sleep took me.

I awoke the next evening to a kiss on my forehead.

"Top," I said as I blinked, "Top?"

"Yes, my lamb. Why you look much better today! As a matter of fact, we were just discussing you. Mater has come to apologize."

I looked over to the fireplace. The old woman's voice trembled as much as her body when she spoke.

"Ruby, you shall live here. And I apologize for striking you."

"That isn't enough," said Top roughly. He tore open the top of her dress, revealing a crooked back with many scars. He positioned her over the top of the winged back chair and took up his riding crop from the nearby table.

"Speak to her without fear, Ruby," said Top.

"What is your name?" I asked the old woman.
"Collette," she answered.
"Don't you ever strike me again Collette."
"I—I wo—won't."
"And this is to make certain of it," growled Top, as he raised the crop. He struck her back five times. That's all it took to make her withered skin crack and bleed. My eyes widened at the sight, but I felt no horror as I looked on. My heart was pounding in my little chest, my palms became wet, and twisted the blanket as a delicious shiver coarsed through me. I licked my lips in nervous satisfaction.

"You turned a blind eye to Ruby's blood," hollered my savior at the woman, "now we shall do the same to yours!" Top seized her by the arm and practically tossed her out of the room. Then he turned to me, tossed the crop back onto the chair, and bowed. I applauded – not in great exuberance, but because now, I had someone to protect me; to hurt those who hurt me. It uncovered an emotion within me that had, until then, had never seen the light of day. It made me feel powerful.

From that day on, Top lavished affection on me. Fabrics, ribbons, sweets and trinkets. He called it, 'worshipping' me. I soon developed a taste for being worshipped. No cooking, no cleaning, no washing. As I blossomed, we made my room into something that would rival *Arabian Nights*. Every inch was bathed in delicious silks and brightly coloured paisley. I was Top's Lady, and I spent my days reading, sewing things for myself, and doing exactly as I pleased.

Mousie, I knew, hated me. She and Collette were nothing but slaves. The two of them could rot for all I cared. All the mattered was that I was finally safe.

*****

"She was attacked by her former lover, you say?" asked Wilkins as he poured us both another coffee, which he had sent up as we sat keeping watch over Ruby and Matthew, both of whom were still slumbering.

"Mad, Wilkins," said I as I held the steaming tin mug carefully. "As mad as the hatter who fashioned that damned blue topper of his. I sent a few men to collect the bodies and bring them here."

"A Workhouse funeral is more than they deserve," said Wilkins, flatly.

"Right you are, Doc," squeaked Matthew.

"How are you feeling, lad?" inquired Wilkins as he walked over to the young man's cat. He felt the patient's forehead and began to take his pulse.

"Other than a bit of fire in my side, I reckon I'm fit," he told the doctor. "I'm obliged to you for saving not only my life, but that of that lovely angel over there."

"My pleasure to do both, Shipmate," answered Wilkins, "And now you'd be obliged to tell me - both of you - just how you came to be in the Charlotte Mews just in time to rescue her?"

Matthew looked over to me. Wilkins's gaze followed.

"Well, Dickens?" said Wilkins in a stern voice.

I took a deep breath, rose, and placed my empty mug upon the table near the door.

"Matthew has been in my employ for some time. He has kept an eye on Ruby since I met her in September."

"It's true, Doc," insisted Matthew, "I offered my services, since I knew her when she was a child. I - I wanted to right the wrong I had done her years ago - mind you, not by my own hand, but by allowing another to harm her. God help me."

"You knew her? What happened? Who harmed her? Top?"

"Long before Top," answered the lad.

Ruby stirred in her sleep. He soft sighs melted each of our chests. Wilkins placed his hand on Matthew's forearm.

"Go on, lad."

"Years ago, her folks gave me a position. An apprenticeship of sorts. They had a small clothing shop. My Master were a tailor; his Missus was a fine milliner. They were good to me. I remember holding Ruby for the first time. So tiny she was! And that smile! But her Pa was thrown from his horse and died. The Missus remarried. He were a fucking brute. It weren't long afore Ruby's Ma was with child. Poor lady suffered greatly in her confinement. Dying in childbirth - her and the babe - were a long overdue mercy. With the wife gone, the brute needed another to torture."

"Ruby?" asked Wilkins.

"No," whispered Matthew. Tears flooded his eyes and he closed them. After several attempts to catch his breath, he surrendered to emotion, and covered his eyes with his arm. He growled at the pain of remembering such a deep trauma.

"Jesus, Matthew," said Wilkins, "he went for you."

"Yet you stayed so he would leave Ruby alone," said I.

"Yes! I was just a child myself. He threatened to take me to Seven Dials and sell me!" ejaculated Matthew in a grating whisper wrought in self loathing. Before us now, Wilkins and I saw the ghost of that vulnerable boy. To harm a child is the greatest crime of all; I struggled not to weep with him.

"I shouldn't have left," he said, his breath now coming in short gasps, "I knew she'd be next. I ran away to sea. Couldn't go home," Matthew continued. He removed his arm from his face.

"Naturally, aye," answered Wilkins with an understanding nod, "if the likes of Top were your kin."

"I came back to see what I could do for Mousie, knowing who she was. But she wanted no saving, and was entirely unworthy of it, anyway. She hated Ruby, and told me how Top spoiled her and gave her fine things. Mousie was left to fend for herself on the street, where she met many types of people. One pal of hers, she said, was going into a house called Urania Cottage."

"That's how you knew about it," I observed.

"Aye," confessed Matthew, "that is how I knew the first time I saw you outside the Rookery that I had to help you; Ruby was in danger."

"Quite so," I continued, "Pity we do not know the identity of Mousie's pal."

"Oh, but we do, Mr. Dickens," said Matthew. "Her name were Mary Anne."

"Oh my God," I cried, and ran my hand through my hair. "That's how Top knew Ruby's every move."

"Matthew," interjected Wilkins, "You know you have to leave England now that you've done murder. The Law won't see it like we do. But I think you can rely on myself and Mr. Dickens not to peach on you."

I nodded. "I swear. The case will grow cold."

"And I still have some contacts who may be able to fix you up a berth with a good Captain."

"Thank you, Doc," said Matthew as he smiled.

"My pleasure," answered the doctor, who was mixing a powder, "Here, drink this."

Matthew did so, and was asleep in minutes. I retrieved my hat and coat, satisfied that justice had been done. But as I opened the door, Wilkins reached over me and, pressing his large hand upon the door, closed it with a thud.

"We are not finished, Dickens."

"Aren't we? All the facts are now known."

"All but the ones that concern you," said the doctor as he removed his hand from the door and placed it heavily upon my shoulder, "You knew she was staying with me."

"Yes. Thanks to Matthew."

"She was in her goddamned petticoats when she arrived at my door, and as frightened as a newborn kitten."

He had me by the lapels now.

"What the fuck did you do to her, you glorified scribbler?"

"Nothing, I assure you. And don't you dare—"

He hurled me against the wall so hard the plaster snowed upon my shoulders.

"WHAT HAPPENED, DICKENS?"

"It was an argument. We both said things we should not have."

"About what?"

I set my jaw as I looked into his eyes. "Kill me if you like. I shall not tell you."

"Joe? Joe?" called a weak voice from behind us. We turned. Ruby's eyes were wide open; they seemed to question whether what they saw were a dream or fact. She took one look at Joe, and held out her hand to him like a small child woken fresh from a nightmare. He was at her side in an instant.

"I'm here, Puss. Don't you cry, darling."

"Oh, Joe," she whimpered. He leaned in and kissed her cheek, whispering sweet words softly in attempt to calm her. I sat on the other side of her bed.

"Ruby, my dear. Forgive me, I beg you. I would do anything to take back the pain I've caused you, please believe that. Katey sends her love to you, and thanks you very much for her dress."

"How did the angel die?" asked Ruby.

She must be asking me about Mary.

"In the arms of one who loved her," I answered, "and still mourns her."

The injured girl regarded me for a moment.

"It was my father-in-law," she eventually said.

"What?" I asked.
"Your casebook."
"What about it?"
She glared at me.

"Get out your damned casebook and write, Goddamn you," she growled. The pain of her shoulder was evident in her voice. I obeyed, and produced my little book. The words that followed had not a trace of emotion. She just said them.

"He was the man who ruined me—against a wall in Brydge's Place. My Pa was a tailor, my Ma a milliner. We had a little place outside of London. Near…Sevenoaks, was it? I cannot even remember, nor do I wish to. I was happy, but I do not wish to remember. Pa died when his horse bolted. Broke his neck. My Ma remarried. The man was a brute. She died in childbirth. He brought me to London. Was going to sell me, but I would not obey. So, he raped me, and left me for dead. Mousie found me and took me to Top. The rest you know."

My pencil had never moved upon the paper. Joe kissed her hand, then her forehead. The love I beheld in her eyes as she looked up at him stirred a thick, heavy envy within me.

"I love you, Joe," she said to the Doctor as she sobbed.

"I love you, Ruby," replied Joe.

"Please don't leave me," she whimpered.

Joe kissed her and quoted Cervantes:

> Or soft or hard, my breast is thine.
> Imprint what characters you will.
> To all eternity divine

Mistress, I'll do your bidding still.

The Lilac Faerie smiled at him through her tears. Then she turned her head toward me.

"You have your story. Now get out."

"Dickens," said Joe, his voice more civil than previously, "I think it best that you heed her request. I will contact you tomorrow."

"Very well," said I, and left the Workhouse as quickly as I could. Once outside the gate, I glanced briefly to my left. Down at the corner, the rooms I had lived in twice as a youth stared back at me. Now Cleveland Street, this had been Norfolk Street then. *I learned to read and write in those rooms.* I began to weep. I turned to my right and walked as if Death were following me. Soon, I was running. My top hat fell from my head. I just kept running.

Mary, my love. Forgive me!

CHAPTER XIV

RETURN TO URANIA.

A knock at the door interrupted Mrs. Fisher as she and the Girls exchanged pleasantries with Wilkins and myself. Mrs. Fisher knew, but the rest would soon realize why the Doctor and I had made conversation in the front passage, and not been shown into the parlour, as was the usual custom.

"Mary Anne," said Mrs. Fisher, "see who that is, will you?"

Joe watched proudly as Ruby's fist met Mary Anne's nose, sending her speedily to the stoop.

"That's for being a peach, you miserable bitch. And as if the Matrons didn't know you were nicking the silver to sell, too."

The smaller girl rose, and Ruby knocked her down again.

"That's for making eyes at my man. I was watching through the window."

I heard Joe suppress a chuckle – only just. The girls, however, cheered Ruby on with vigor.

"Knock her on her ass again, Ruby!"

"You cun—" Mary Anne tried to finish her small sentence as she swung. But her broken nose obscured her vision. She spun clean around in a circle as Ruby ducked and came up, her fist striking its target a third time.

"And that's for your bloody awful dress sense."

Mary Anne lay upon the ground, barely coherent as Ruby rubbed her hands together and turned to the

Police, who had rounded the corner from their agreed upon hiding place.

"Gents, she's all yours," said Ruby with a graceful curtsey that was worthy of Her Majesty's Royal Court. Those men tipped their caps to her, not pretending to hide their amusement at the scene they had just witnessed. I gestured for Ruby to enter.

"I enjoyed that," said Ruby with vigor. "So, Ladies. What's for tea, then?"

The girls flew toward Ruby, surrounding her with welcomes and embraces.

*****

My hand buzzed as if I had rammed it into a beehive. Then, for the first and last time, Mrs. Holdsworth smiled at me. Mrs. Fisher embraced me, then did Julia, who was fighting back tears. The rest of the lot were chirping out questions, wanting to know all about what had happened to me.

"Now, now, girls," said Dickens, "Let us adjourn to the parlour."

Dickens and the Matrons left the foyer. There had been a new addition to the fold in the weeks I was gone.

"Where you from, then?" I asked her.

"The Madeleine," she responded. "That Doctor your friend?"

"Yeah," I answered point of fact, "what of it?"

"Christ," exclaimed the new girl in a hushed voice, "he's gorgeous! Caw, I do believe I'm feeling a bout of hysteria coming on, if you take my meaning. Think he'd fancy being our house doctor?"

I smiled, rested my left hand on her shoulder and squeezed.

"Touch him and I'll slit you from cunt to collarbone with a knitting pin," I whispered back.

"Push off. You don't frighten me," said Emma.

I grabbed her by the front of her dress.

"Listen and listen well—the Thames couldn't best me. A bullet couldn't best me. And you aren't going to best me. Have a care where you cast your eyes, lest you wake up without them. Remind me to tell you someday about how my last lover went blind. Are we clear, my love?"

The other girls were giggling. And as extra humiliation for Emma, I licked her cheek. She shrugged out of my hands and quickly went into the parlour.

Joe made his way over to me, and all the girls gave him the eye. But he kept his eyes on me. Julia kissed my cheek and took my bonnet and shawl. I looked down at my gloves; there was blood on the right hand knuckles. Joe tenderly took my hand in his.

"Let me take this off," he whispered.

Though I smiled coyly, I momentarily forgot how to breathe. Oh God, how I wanted him to take off more than my gloves. But Dickens had insisted that Joe and I behave as friends and nothing more while I lived under Urania's roof. I had never had to wait for a man; anything or anyone I wanted had always been easily and quickly attained.

Why didn't someone tell me that romance was agony?

"Would one of you fine lasses fetch a bit of ice for Ruby's hand, please?" cooed Joe.

"A fair amount is still left in the ice box. It would be my pleasure, Doctor," replied Julia, who made for the kitchen.

"Here, I'll take them gloves. They'll need sponging off," said Rosie, who took them and exited the foyer.

Joe and I were alone now. We had only a few moments. I looked up at the man whom I had grown to love with all my body and soul, and my eyes filled.

"I'm not ready to do this," I said to Joe, my voice small and unsure.

"Neither am I," answered my darling, "but we must. You will do fine here, darling. And my sister needs me now."

The harder I tried, the more I couldn't stop the tears. I fell into his arms.

"Write to me?" I said into his jacket.

"Every week. I promise," said Joe. He kissed the top of my head and held me close, careful of my shoulder, though it was nearly healed.

"I love you."

"I love you."

I reached up and guided his lips to mine. It didn't last long enough for me, and as he pulled away, I pulled him back. But he cupped my face in his hands.

"There'll be more time for kissing soon enough, Puss. Don't worry."

He wiped way my tears with his handkerchief. Then picked up his hat and coat and made to the door. I did not want to let him go. I wanted to ask him, beg him to take me with him. But as tempting as that offer would have been, I had fallen in love with a man of honour. Nothing would make him go back on his promise to let me finish my time here.

"Joe," I called.

"Go inside and get ice on that hand," he said as he put his coat, "That's an order, Puss."

I giggled through my tears, "Aye aye, Boots."

He opened the door, blew me a kiss and winked. The pain of leaving me was there in his eyes, but so was the love he had for this unworthy girl. The door closed behind him.

Right, now the work begins. So pull yourself together and get on with it, Ruby.

I put head in my hands and sobbed as silently as I could manage. Then, after three deep, heaving breaths, I wiped my eyes and pinched my cheeks. I took one last deep breath for luck and opened the parlour doors. Dear Rex chirruped a hearty 'Hallo!' as I entered, smiling.

CHAPTER XXV

FAREWELL, URANIA.

The next two months passed as quickly as they could. For the first of them, Joe's absence was nearly too much to bear. All day long, I would store the tears like rain in a barrel. Then, when the house was dark, I would let them drip as silently as I could, and float upon them to sleep. As always, Julia was very obliging.

Joe wrote to me every week. Because we knew Mrs. Holdsworth would read each of the letters, he kept them short. But it was no matter; I did not need endless declarations of love. I knew he was mine, and would wait for me.

I found that the best cure for my loneliness (other than the times when Julia left me alone in our room to quickly relieve myself—my need was great at first, but mercifully tapered as I settled back into life at the cottage) was work. What had once been tedium and dull, senseless drudgery now seemed a blessing. It was not long before I found myself harmonizing with the daily tasks of cooking and cleaning. I will not say I loved it all, but I will say that I hated it all, either.

Dickens visited as often as he could, but not as frequently as he had done at first. We still enjoyed lively chats, and I made good on Miss Katey's dress—he had it all sent to Urania to be finished. When I suggested that all the girls should help with it, he smiled brightly.

"A marvelous idea, dear girl! Indeed, it would be good experience for them to learn about children's clothes."

Being more adept at sewing than many of the other girls, I found I enjoyed teaching them. Soon they were good enough that I could read aloud as they worked, with only an occasional call of, "Sorry Ruby, love. How do I does this bit again?"

Men had worshipped me, adored me, possessed me. But until I met Dickens and Joe, none had ever respected me. And now, these girls respected me. Fellow whores and criminals—some of whom had had much harder lives than mine—respected me. What was more, I respected myself. I wrote of this to Joe, and his responses of pride and encouragement meant the world to me.

March of 1849 arrived sooner than I had anticipated. My time at Urania was over. This day I was on my way to board a ship called, *Posthumous*, bound for Port Adelaide, Australia. Julia and others had left in January aboard *Calcutta*. I own it was a tearful goodbye on both our parts.

Rosie and Emma (another of many girls that had come to Urania during my time there) had already gone out to the carriage. Mrs. Holdsworth and Mrs. Furze (the shrew who had replaced Mrs. Fisher when she fell in love and left to be married) had already said their goodbyes to me. That left Dandy and myself alone in the parlour save for dear little Rex, who was busy eating the crumbs we had lavished upon him as a farewell gift.

"I have a gift for you," said Dickens as he handed me a small parcel. I opened it to find a long length of inch thick lilac ribbon of the purest satin.

"From Miss Coutts and myself, of course," he winked.

"Of course," I said as I smiled, "Please thank her for me."

"I will. They are going to miss you here, you know."

"I shall miss them."

"Truly?"

"Yes. I might even miss you."

"Ruby, I am so sorr—"

I put my hand to his lips.

"Please don't. That's all past now."

He held my fingers to his lips a moment longer and kissed them softly.

"I see Mary's shadow in you, I do not deny it."

"She would be proud of this house, I'm sure of it," I said, and meant it.

"My dear girl," he said as his hand stroked my cheek, "I shall miss you more than you know."

"You're a strange one and mistake, Dandy."

He laughed and pulled me, by my consent, into his arms. There was no passion or ardor; we held one another as a brother and sister.

"Oh, Ruby," whispered Dickens, "you have brought such light to this little Home, not to mention to my heart. Thank you for helping me to prove this idea of mine was a good one."

"It was my pleasure," I replied. His elegant green paisley waistcoat smelled sweetly of candle smoke.

He held me close for one more brief moment. Then he released me, but held my hand in his. The famous author, my friend, bowed and kissed my hand as if I were Victoria herself.

"Farewell, Lilac," he said tenderly. The glow in his face and magnificent eyes were as proud as the sun.

"Farewell, Dandy," I answered.

He walked me out to the waiting carriage. I looked up to see Matthew as the driver, smiling proudly.

"Matthew!" I cried with delight.

He winked and tipped his hat to me as Dickens helped me in.

"Where to, Ladies?" asked Matthew.

"Australia!" we shouted in unison.

"Right. Hear that, horses? Can you swim?"

"Good luck, Ladies!" said Dickens in a hearty voice. He smiled proudly at his second round of graduates.

As we sped away en route to Gravesend, Emma looked back. We had become good pals over the last few months. Dickens had been very strict with her. But unlike Mary Anne, she had come around. Now, this girl whom I had once threatened leaned her head on my shoulder and cried unabashedly. I put my arm around her.

"Be proud, Em. We did it!"

"I am proud. It's just that that was the first home I ever really had."

"Now we'll make the *Posthumous* our home for a few months," said Rosie, "You been on a ship before, Ruby?"

"No. But we'll manage."

I pulled Emma a little closer and rubbed her back with my palm. My head remained high; I did not look back.

I would never look back again.

CHAPTER XXVI

NEW HORIZONS.

Dickens neglected to inform us of the intolerable cold we would find when we reached Port Adelaide. It had taken about a fortnight for me to get my sea-legs after we left Gravesend. Emma had taken a bit longer. Rosie's sea-legs never arrived at all, but she pressed on despite it. For the first few weeks, we would rise, vomit, wash our faces, get dressed, vomit, take breakfast, vomit, read, vomit, have a lie down, vomit, sew for a while, vomit, forego any further meals and retire to bed by tea time. Emma and I took turns caring for Miss Morris, our chaperone. She was a pleasant, elderly woman. The poor thing got out of her bunk only when absolutely necessary.

For three months, our home was a tiny cabin with four tiny bunks. Before leaving Urania, Rosie, Emma and I had each been allowed to pack two small dresses and several chemises (which we had made) into our trunks, a gift from Miss Coutts, who had also paid for the tickets. In addition, Miss Coutts saw to it that we had cakes of soap, sheets, towels, bedding and a 'mess'—a tin cup, plate, fork, knife and spoon. We were also given two pairs of shoes. It was a generous reward for our time at the Home, and we had each written letters to Miss Coutts which I handed off to Matthew one day when our ship hailed one bound back to England.

The chill of March gave way to the balmy countenance of April and May. By June, however, the kiss of Summertime was sorely lacking. The air became frigid below decks. We girls took care of one another as we never had before—keeping clean, making sure we all ate (even if it came back up), and taking regular turns on deck. Joe, in a letter he had written to me while I was still at Urania, had advised that we walk amidships, or as closest to the main mast as we could.

That big branchless tree in the middle, darling. That's the one to be near. Square your shoulders and stare at the horizon. Breathe in the good sea air. It will not fail you. The air below decks will no doubt become foul, so come up as often as you are able. And when you feel the breeze tickle your cheek, well, that's a kiss I have sent upon its obliging wings.

Now, finally at our destination, the crew was making the ship fast to the dock. Miss Morris remained below with Rosie. Emma and I had come up on deck to watch the men work.

"What do you mean the *Calcutta* hasn't arrived yet, Matthew? She set sail five months ago—that's two more than it took us to get here!"

"Rub—er, um, Miss Waller," said Matthew (who had gotten a berth as an Able Bodied Seaman) as he coiled a line on the deck, "that is what is reported. I don't know no more than that."

"Keep trying, Matthew."

"You know I will. Word will come soon, don't worry. How—How's Miss Emma today?"

"Why don't you ask her yourself, Sailor?" answered Emma, standing behind him inside the neatly coiled circle of line. Matthew had explained that we mustn't call it rope for reasons that only a sailor cares about.

"Miss Emma," said Matthew, alarmed as he picked her up out of instinct and set her next to me, "you should never step inside a coil. You could end up like a rabbit in a snare, if you're lucky. You could end up losing a leg if you're not."

Emma blushed, "I'm so sorry, Matthew. Thank you for making sure I didn't come to any harm."

"I'd never let any harm come to you, Miss Emma," returned Matthew, with a respectful tip of his cap. He looked very robust and handsome in his ink blue broad falls, black short coat and blue check shirt, both of which were open enough to reveal the hair of his chest.

"Emma, let the poor man be about his duties," I interrupted, "We must pack. I am not spending another second on this hulk longer than I have to."

Emma blew a kiss to Matthew, who caught it with his hand. He then gathered up the coil. Had he actually been watching what he was doing rather than copping an eye full of Emma, the coil might just have made it to its proper belaying pin. Instead, it collapsed like a drunken snake back on the deck. We walked away from him, giggling like schoolgirls.

"He's sweet on you," I teased.

"I know. He's nice," said Emma as she looped her arm in mine.

"Wish my man was here," I said.

"He'll be here, Ruby," said Emma as we reached the companionway.

"Em, I miss him so much," I said.

Miss Morris was in no condition to be moved. We were invited to stay aboard another night together. We had packed our humble trunks, save what we would need for morning, so our departure would be swift. The cold was such that we slept in our clothes, so no extra time would be allotted for dressing in the morning.

By next afternoon, I could stand it no longer. Rosie (snoring in the top bunk opposite mine) could have slept through the second coming of Christ, so she didn't hear me rise. I think Miss Morris noticed, but she said nothing. Emma was still asleep in the bunk above mine.

I rose as quietly as I could and made my way on deck, quickly donning my bonnet and shawl in the passageway before ascending the companionway. As I looked out onto the quayside, I saw no familiar faces. I leaned against the pin rail and closed my eyes.

Joe, where are you? Your ship was supposed to arrive yesterday! Oh my darling, if something has happened to you...

A pair of arms tenderly entwined about my waist.

"Ahoy, Miss Puss."

His lips pressed against my neck. I closed my eyes and let out a sob that probably woke all of Port Adelaide.

"Joe!" I turned and threw my arms about his neck. He picked me up off the deck and twirled me. We kissed each other's face and lips all over until we were both gasping for breath. Eventually, I pulled back and looked at him. He looked very well. His fine, full cheeks were more ruddy than usual.

"Sorry we're late, darling," he finally said. He was panting from our kissing. I put my hands on his velvet coat lapels and savored the heaving of his chest. He guided me to the starboard rail. Julia, Jane and Martha (two more Urania girls) were waving from the quayside.

"It was a ghastly crossing," said Joe, "but they did well. There was no doubt we would make it. It was just a question of when. The girls hardly needed my assistance at all."

They had all sailed aboard *Calcutta* together back in January. Dickens had insisted for form's sake that Joe and I make the crossing on separate ships. At first I had been insulted, as he and Miss Coutts secretly knew that Joe and I intended to marry as soon as we reached Australia. I felt it cruel to be parted from Joe for so many long months. But Miss Coutts explained to me that it was all for the best. Reluctantly, I had resigned myself to the bargain.

"My sister sends her best," said Joe.

"Good. I still can't believe you sold your practice to come and be with me," I said to Joe.

"Ruby Waller, I would follow you to hell itself."

"No thank you. Our marriage bed shall be hot enough!"

"Right you are, my love. Well, look alive, Puss! Rouse the other girls and let's be off. Then you and I are going to find a church."

That night, Joe and I lay in each other's arms as man and wife. We had a small private cabin aboard a steamship bound for Boston. After three months at sea already, only my husband could have persuaded me to board another ship.

Joe had relatives in America. A cousin of his, also a doctor, had written to Joe asking him to open a practice with him. I longed to see the latest fashions in such a city. During the voyage aboard *Posthumous*, I had acquired copy of Dickens's *American Notes* by teaching a sailor how to knit a shawl for his lady friend. If Dandy thought well of Boston, I was certain I would like it there.

I had wept openly when I had said goodbye to my girls. So had they. I embraced them all, along with Matthew (who decided to remain in Adelaide for an extended visit), wishing them lives full of happiness. Knowing that in all likelihood we would never see one another again was almost too much to bear. But I was also about to be a bride—what just cause did I have to grieve?

Joe had looked at me with such love as I pledged to be his wife. Before he slid it onto my finger, he kissed the small gold ring that had belonged to his dear mother. I was proud to wear it.

For me, our first lovemaking had been like learning a new language. However, after our subsequent tumults, it was a language I knew I would master easily. I sighed contentedly as I lay atop Joe's chest. My hair served as a blanket for us;

the exquisite heat of our passion had caused the woolen blankets to be thrown to the floor, where they now rested, entwined with our clothes.

God, if you do exist, thank you for giving me Joe.

"Are you alright?" asked my husband.

I turned my face and kissed his chest.

"I'm quite well, Doctor," I teased as I looked up at him, "thank you."

Joe bent his head down and kissed me.

"I love you," he whispered.

"And I don't deserve you," I answered, my voice full of emotion.

"That's true. You don't," he joked.

I sat up and pretended to pummel him. He laughed and reached up to tickle my sides. When sat up and put his mouth on my breast, my giggles swiftly turned to moaning. He pulled me back down and lay atop me.

"When we get to Boston, Puss," he said as he looked down at me and stroked my hair, "I'm going to spoil you."

I opened my thighs and ran my hands through his hair.

"That's Mrs. Puss to you, Boots."

CHAPTER XXVII

MECHANIC'S HALL. WORCESTER, MASS.
23 MARCH, 1868

White globed gaslights shone overhead as we entered, giving the white walls, mahogany bannisters and brass fixtures a clean, inviting glow. We ascended one of two grand, crimson-carpeted staircases. They were wide, with more than enough room for a couple to walk together, even with Ladies in their fine, flowing hoops. These stairs led to the second floor, which had a grand balcony and several doors leading to a large hall.

The closer we got to the doors, the more a foul scent overtook us.

"Joe, what's that pong?" I asked quietly.

"It's chicken shit," he answered.

"It's so bad it nearly makes me homesick for the Thames."

I put my handkerchief to my face, thankful I had severely doused it with orange flower water before leaving the hotel. Joe and I looked at each other with puzzled faces. A moment later, a door opened. A young usher with butter colored hair and pimples quickly exited, followed by a trail of white and brown feathers. He went rushing past us, limping a bit and muttering under his breath.

"Here, lad," said Joe to him, "what goes on in there?"

"Poultry show, Sir," said the young man, his voice still cracking due to his delicate years,

"Mr. Dickens' performance is up the stairs."

"You poor boy. Got your ankles, didn't they?" I observed.

"And if it were up to me I'd fry the lot of them and be done with it!" exclaimed the lad. Then off he stomped, trailing chicken feathers in his wake.

I held my husband's arm while we ascended the second set of crimson-carpeted steps. At the top, there were more steps to either side, with yet more leading to the main hall where Dickens was to perform.

The hall was vast and full of light. A second tier ran the length of three sides. The massive paneled walls bore large, gold framed portraits. At the back of center stage, great white Grecian pillars framed a mighty set of organ pipes. In addition to footlights, the stage was dressed only by a maroon curtain and a small, oddly shaped desk at the center front, with one side lower than the other. The desk was bound in the same maroon fabric as the curtain, trimmed with gold fringe and studded with large tacks. The table had a lamp, a water carafe and glass, and a bone letter opener perched upon it.

As Joe and I found our seats (which were in the center, four rows back), I noticed that the floor boards, which were not tightly aligned in some areas, allowed the sounds and smells of the feathered prisoners below to waft up. Though the odor was not overpowering, I kept my handkerchief handy.

Soon a man came on stage and turned up the gas lights. The audience fell silent and still, waiting for the great novelist to emerge. But no sooner had the lamps shone bright than a symphony of raucous cock-a-doodle-do's and obnoxious clucks fit to make a banshee turn in her shroud assaulted the main hall. I burst into a fit of giggles, all the while Joe trying to hush me without succumbing to it himself.

"Joe," I said, "there must be a thousand chickens down in that bloody room!"

"And now they all think that it's morning! Can't say much for New England ingenuity," he mused. "Do you want to leave, Ruby?"

"Not on your life. Wild horses couldn't drag me from this!" I said, and kissed his cheek, not giving a damn for propriety.

I propped my foot on the leg of the chair in front of me as Joe looked at his pocket watch. It was eight o'clock precisely. A white curtain moved to the left of the stage. An old, bearded man with thinning grey hair combed in great gusts about his head ascended the steps onto the stage. The hall erupted with applause, temporarily surpassing the ardor of the chickens.

Dandy? What the hell has happened to you?

The cuffs, a bit too long for the cut of the sleeve, the red geranium, the thick gold watch chain still did not convince me. He still wore that ring on his little finger. Then the old man looked out at his audience. As if he were surveying virgin land, he took his time. The once nubile face was deeply creased, like a shoe after many years of hard use.

Those eyes, though I had not beheld them in nineteen years, were still as luminous as the night we first met. I would have known them anywhere. As they passed across mine, my breath caught in my breast. It was him.

Still a Dandy. But my God, how you've aged. But I see your dress sense has not.

The gaslight must have blinded him; for he gave no recognition of knowing me. His eyes moved to Joe, and then beyond. Heedless of the caterwauling poultry below, Dickens began.

"Marley was dead, to begin with..."

His voice was husky; as if he were battling a cold. I relaxed in my seat and tried to concentrate. But talk of Scrooge, Marley and Bob Cratchit was quickly drowned by a thousand memories that flooded into my senses. I heard nothing; I was back on that doorstep in Southwark, kissing that fresh faced young man, my half frozen fingers devouring his exquisite, wild hair and caressing the smooth skin on the back of his neck. The next thing I remember, the audience was applauding. I caught a glimpse of Dickens's tailcoat as he left the stage.

"Is it over, Joe?" I asked worriedly.

"Just the interval," he said.

The second act was much like the first. Dickens had us all weeping at Tiny Tim's death and Scrooge's salvation. Then he did the trial scene from *The Pickwick Papers*. Penned over three decades before, it was met with great enthusiasm. Joe and I laughed just as hard as everyone else at the impressions of Sergeant Buzfuzz and the ever popular Sam Weller. I think even the chickens liked it.

At the conclusion, Dickens took the thunderous ovation with the grace of an emperor. He now turned his attention to the edge of the stage. Ladies had left small floral testimonials there. They were each adorned with different ribbons. Some even had small cards attached. He picked them up, bowed gracefully, and left the stage.

Ever the Gentleman, Dandy. Ever the Showman!

Joe and I filed out with the crowd. As we passed the stage, I reached up and caressed the smooth wood with my gloved hand as we walked toward the door.

"Do you think he saw us?" I asked my husband.

"The lamps are very bright. It is doubtful he knew it was us," Joe answered.

"He didn't look well at all," I observed.

"He's not," answered Joe.

CHAPTER XXVIII

AN AFTERNOON WALK IN ROCHESTER.
JUNE, 1870

A return to England meant a return to the lush, rolling, green countryside of my all but forgotten childhood. At last, I was amongst the flowers and trees of my shrouded memories. Since my attacks of gout had left me years before, I had developed a love of walking. We had taken a small cottage in Kent. It was just the two of us, as all our travels had been throughout America. Though not from want of effort, there had never been children. But as I never considered myself the ideal candidate for Motherhood (nor was I in the least bit interested), I was more than content to have my man all to myself.

This day I was returning from fitting a woman for a party dress. Joe had driven me in our small carriage. Along a stretch of road, I saw a man leaning against the stone wall, clutching his left leg. His back was to us, but he was wearing checked trousers with a wide black stripe down the sides, a black bowler and jacket, immaculately shined boots, and had grey, grizzled hair.

Ever the physician, Joe stopped the horse. I got out first and approached the man. As I got closer, I saw a pair of canary gloves sticking out of his coat pocket. A small ring, well known to me in years past, rested upon his little finger.

"Dandy?" I called softly.

The man turned to face me. His eyes searched mine, as if he were trying to place me. I held my breath as I had at Mechanics Hall.

"Ruby," said a breathless Charles Dickens.

"Aye!" I said as I smiled and I clutched his hand. *Christ, he's in real pain.*

"Good God. You're—you're in England!" he looked like a little boy who found an empty stocking at Christmas, and about to burst into tears.

I removed my left glove to take his pulse, as Joe had taught me.

"I'll explain later. What in hell happened to you?"

My aged Dandy made to answer. But it was then that he spotted my wedding ring. He shuddered an intake of breath, and his eyes looked at me with a melancholy that broke my heart.

"Joseph Wilkins is a fortunate man," he said.

"Indeed I am," answered my husband.

Dickens looked over at him and gave a weary laugh. In that moment, the young man I had known showed himself once more.

"What brought this attack on, Dickens?" asked Joe.

"Oh, just too much walking, I suppose," he said as he patted his left thigh, "This damned leg."

"What's wrong with it?" I asked.

"It thinks it's older than the rest of me."

"Don't be coy, Dandy. Remember I've had bouts with the gout, too."

"Wilkins," Dickens laughed, "you have made a nurse out of her."

I smiled wiped a bit of sweat off his brow with my handkerchief, "Why don't you ride a horse?"

"Sometimes I do. But you know my penchant for walking."

"You was younger then, Charles," I said.

"God," he exclaimed as he rolled his eyes, "please don't remind me."

"Is there someone we can fetch for you?" I interjected.

"Just get me to the Falstaff Inn, if you please. They can send word from there."

It took no more than a few minutes to reach the Falstaff Inn. Dandy greeted the barkeep as Joe helped him to sit down. Then he went to fetch a brandy.

"Thank you both," said the aged author. "May I buy you both a drink?"

"That is very kind of you, but we must get to a patient."

"Yes of course," answered Dickens.

"How's Mrs. Dickens?" I asked.

"Well," he answered, "thank you. At least, she was when I last received a letter from her."

"Letter? Oh, she's abroad, then?"

"I no longer reside in London," he answered, his mood sinking slightly.

"Oh, I see," I said, thinking it best not to pry.

His bowed his head. For a moment, I thought he was going to cry. I reached down to his lap (a former whore never forgets) and patted his hand. I began to twist that dear little ring on his finger. He looked over at me. The gaze with which we regarded one another spoke of a bond no other human being could ever understand. Not Joe. Not Mary. Just my Dandy and I. Fleeting yet none the less heartfelt, we were together again.

"I never told Joe about Mary," I whispered.

Dickens closed his eyes and nodded his thanks fervently. I knew he was trying desperately not to weep.

"I've kept up with your books," I said, in an attempt to change the subject.

His eyes opened wide.

"You have?" Dickens asked with a proud smile.

"Aye. *Little Dorrit* was excellent. One of your best, if you ask me. I liked Amy very much. Rigaud was a capital villain. And those ungrateful siblings—" I said, wrinkling my nose in disgust.

"And *Copperfield*? Did—did you read *David Copperfield*?" he asked.

I nodded.

"Superb, Dandy. Superb. In truth, I was more partial to *Little Dorrit*. But yes, you did Em'ly and Martha up a treat. Bravo. I cried when I read of Em'ly's rescue."

Dickens's eyes welled up.

"Thank you for helping me to pen it."

Then the great author bowed to me.

"A favorable critique from a true authority," he said with a wink, "Mrs. Wilkins, you do me honour. Please, do come to my house, Gad's Hill. Let's make it soon. Stay for a few days. You both would be more than welcome!"

"Welcome where?" asked Joe pleasantly, who had only just returned to the table. He handed Dickens the glass.

"Gad's Hill, Doctor. My home. Please say you will be my guests for at least a week."

"We'd love to, I'm sure, Charles," I answered before Joe could speak. I was so happy to see Dickens more exuberant than when we first saw him along the road that I couldn't have refused. My husband nodded in agreement. He knew he wasn't getting out of this, and I knew he'd do it out of love for me.

"I'm certain my patients will last for a few days without me. Summer can be a dull season for doctors. When would be convenient to call?"

Dickens took a long sip of brandy.

"Oh, I should think preparations could be made by Thursday. Let's make it the ninth."

CHAPTER XXIX

COMINGS AND PARTINGS.
9 JUNE, 1870

Gad's Hill was not a large mansion. We were surprised to see several carriages out in front of the house. There was a man smoking a cigar out on the front steps.

"I am sorry, but you cannot enter," he said.

"We were expected today by Mr. Dickens," said Joe.

"Mr. Dickens had a stroke yesterday evening."

"Is he dead?" I asked.

"It will not be long."

Joe put his arm around me.

"We are old friends of his," I said. "I am a graduate of Urania Cottage."

"I am sorry, Ma'am, but you cannot—"

"Lilac!" called a woman's voice from inside the foyer as she emerged into the June sun. It was Katey. She held out her arms and I ran to her side. We held each other tightly for at least a minute.

"Oh, Dearie," I whispered. She swallowed, drew a hard breath, and looked at me.

"Take me to him."

Katey nodded and motioned for Joe to follow us. She led us into a room. There, in the presence of family and several doctors, on an emerald chaise longue, lay poor Charles. I knelt down close to him.

"Dandy, it's Lilac. I kept our appointment this time. Joe's here, too."

He did not answer. I touched his face, which was wet with tears. Joe guided me to a chair behind Katey. We sat in silence for several moments. Suddenly, as the dying author drew a deep breath, so did those assembled to bid him farewell. Then, he exhaled, and one more tear travelled down his pale, exhausted cheek. Joe squeezed my hand. It was over. From different parts of the room, the weeping began. I did not cry, but I laid my head on Joe's shoulder. I noticed a young woman of soft features and fair hair sitting very still, watching me from the far corner of the room. One look told me she was not one of his daughters. When my eyes met hers, she rose and quietly left the room. No one seemed to notice. I rose, and followed her into the garden.

"He loves flowers," she said as she leaned against a stone wall.

"I know. I'm Ruby."

"I know. I'm Nellie. What else do you know?" she asked.

"That you're in a great more pain that you want them to know," I said as I gestured toward the door.

"He was right. You look very much like her."

"I know," I responded. "He loved you."

"How do you know that? Did he tell you?"

"No. But you are not a relative, and I know his fancies. I've known Charles for many years."

"So have I," said the girl, wearily. "And the man who is accompanying you?" inquired Nellie, desperate to change the subject, "Who is he?"

"Doctor Wilkins. My husband," I said rather proudly, "You could say that we met through Charles's intervention."

"Oh," she simply said as she touched a rose on the nearby trellis. Her blue eyes were brimmed with tears. "Yes, he likes to intervene." Suddenly, her hand began to falter and she seized the rose, tearing it from its stem. She regarded it in her hand, then with a cry of anguish threw it to the ground and began to sob. I went to her, but she pushed me away.

"I don't need your pity!" she said.

"Good, because I have none to give," I answered as I rested my spare handkerchief on the grass beside her. She snatched it up and buried her face in it.

"I know what they all think of me," rasped the girl. "The poor little actress. The, the—"

"Whore?"

Nellie cried harder at that.

"Nellie."

She would not look up.

"Darling, please look at me."

Nellie did not respond. I seized her shoulders and shook with all my strength.

"Look at me, goddammit!"

She did so that time.

"I was a whore, Nellie. A selfish, scheming whore. As a girl I was raped and cast out on the streets. There was a time when I didn't think I'd ever escape it. Do you judge me?"

"No," she sniffed, "I am sure you did what you had to in order to survive."

"Exactly," I said, looking deeply into her eyes, "It's what we women must do sometimes."

Her face flashed in recognition of my words. Then it flashed a question, "Did—did you and Charles?"

I laughed. "No." I reached out my hands to her, and helped her to stand, "Take a bit of advice?"

"Very well," she answered nervously.

I framed her face in my hands.

"Hold your head high, Nellie."

She laughed through her tears, "A professional's opinion."

I kissed her forehead, then reached into my reticule and handed her a calling card.

"If you wish to talk to someone who will understand, you may write or call upon me at any time."

"Thank you," said the girl. She kissed my cheek.

We went back inside Gad's Hill. Joe was in the doorway, and I walked into his waiting embrace. Nellie reclaimed her chair, and Katey looked at me. I winked at her, and she gave me a small smile as I kept my cheek on Joe's chest.

"We should take our leave, Ruby," said my husband. "The family has much to do. Go say your goodbyes."

Joe then left the room. I approached and knelt before Charles's body, and beheld his face for the last time. His face had begun to relax, and the valleys of worry which had creased his skin were fading in death. I gently kissed his lips.

"Goodbye, Dandy," I whispered. Then I walked to Katey and Mamie, and embraced each of them.

Nellie approached, and I held her for a time in my arms as well. Miss Georgina stared at us. I offered my hand to her, which she graciously took. I voiced my condolences to all and then, with one last curtsey, I took my leave of the Dickens family, Gad's Hill, and the man who had altered my life forever.

EPILOGUE

I stood next to her, though she could not see me. Ruby, I knew you were there at my side at Gad's Hill, but could not answer.

How kind the years have been to you! Still an ethereal vision; still so tiny, still so perfect. My heart has ceased to beat, yet I can feel it soar and flutter as I behold you. It was good of you to come. Would that we could have that last chat here...now. I would tell you so many things...

I did not want to be buried here. They did it anyway. I own you were correct when you said it was not a bad place to spend eternity, but give me the peace of Rochester Cathedral any day!

You have tossed flowers upon my grave. Lilacs. Ha! I would have expected no other. But, hold, there is a missive attached.

> She smiles preferment, or she frowns disgrace,
> Curtsies a pension here—there nods a place.
> Nor with less awe, in scenes of humbler life,
> Is view'd the mistress, or is heard the wife.
> The poorest peasant of the poorest soil,
> The child of poverty, and heir to toil,
> Early from radiant Love's impartial light
> Steals one small spark to cheer this world of night:
> Dear spark! that oft through winter's chilling woes
> Is all the warmth his little cottage knows!

The Rivals! My eyes are blurred. Sheridan was an excellent choice, my dear.

You have paid your respects, yet you remain. Why? Do you sense me, I wonder? Dare I kiss your cheek? Aye, I dare! Oh, you shiver. You know I am near, Ruby! Yes, look in my direction. I am right here. Shall we away together for a gin somewhere? What times we had, eh? You were so young and headstrong; I so cocksure and foolish.

Enough. It is all past. Go, Ruby – I see Joe standing by a pillar, keeping a respectful distance. You wanted to do this alone, didn't you? The love in his eyes has not altered by time; how proud he is to call you his wife!

Go, Ruby, my darling Lilac Faerie, to the waiting arms of your husband. Mary calls now, and bids me to thank you. I must go now as well. Farewell, Ruby, my children, Farewell All, my Dear Ones!

May it please God to say I left the human race better than when I arrived among them. Let the world judge me by my published works. Let history know that Ruby Waller made me a better writer...a better man.

If I keep telling myself that, perhaps history shall record it as truth.

FINIS.

Historical Note

According to Jenny Hartley's book, *Charles Dickens and the House of Fallen Women*, Rubina Waller disappeared from public record as soon as she arrived in Australia. It was recorded that her father in law was 'bad'. The girls of Urania Cottage and their matrons were real, though I have embellished them.

While Dickens did personally interview girls for Urania, the nature of Dickens's relationship with Ruby is fiction (though she was at Tothill Fields). There is also no known likeness of Rubina Waller. I created her resemblance to Mary Hogarth to delve deeper into Dickens's mind, as I did the conversations with his real friend, John Forster. Angela Burdett Coutts was the patroness of Urania Cottage, though the conversations depicted in this novel come from my imagination. I found a letter he wrote to her in Edgar Johnson's *The Heart of Charles Dickens* (1952). It said of the Urania project, "I know the idea is a good one, because it is mine."

Mrs. Dickens, the children, Georgina Hogarth, and Nellie Ternan appear briefly, and I hope I have done them justice. Save for them, Dr. Joseph Wilkins, Top, Collette, Mousie, Matthew and the others are my own creation.

Acknowledgements

I would be remiss if I did not first thank Charles Dickens and Rubina Waller, without whom this novel would never have been born.

To my parents Chuck and Marian Emerson, who instilled a love of Dickens in my heart at the tender age of seven. Special thanks to Dr. Michael C. White, creator and Director of the MFA Creative Writing Program at Fairfield University. Michael, thank you for helping me find my courage. To Bill Patrick, Da Chen, Hollis Seamon, Joan Connor, Lary Bloom, Baron Wormser, Elizabeth "Mother" Hastings, Kathy Doornbosch, Lisa Deeds, Teya King, and all of my mentors, colleagues and friends in the Creative Writing Program at Fairfield University. To two wonderful friends: my patient and supportive co-designer, Mark Roberts, and his wife, Native American Medicine Woman, Leslie Karen Hammond.

To Elaine Bentley Baughn, my fabulous reader and friend. To Kevin Quinn, Mike and Su Quinn and everyone at the Friends of Dickens New York. Bill Kelleher and everyone at the Connecticut Branch of the Dickens Fellowship. Dr. Ruth Richardson, whose love and knowledge of 'our' beloved London is a rare gem to be treasured, and to whom the chapters at The George and Strand Union Workhouse are dedicated. The character of Dr. Wilkins was inspired by her love for and efforts to save Strand Union Workhouse (now Cleveland Street Workhouse), and perpetuate the memory of its real life Medical Officer, Dr. Joseph Rogers,

M.D. To Professor Jenny Hartley, current President of the International Dickens Fellowship, whose book *Charles Dickens and the House of Fallen Women* was of inestimable value to me. To David Perdue and his most excellent website! To Lucinda Dickens Hawksley – your encouragement means more than you know. Emma King and everyone at the Charles Dickens House Museum, London. Thank you for making this Little Connecticut Yankee feel so welcome! To Susan Graham, my harp teacher and friend. All my friends at Mystic Seaport, the Shaw Mansion, the Lucretia Shaw Chapter of the Daughters of the American Revolution, the Friends of Fort Griswold, SubVets Groton Base, the Avery-Copp House Museum, the Denison Homestead and the Smith-Harris House. To Matthew Stackpole for his unceasing and utterly contagious support and enthusiasm. To Laurie and Joe Ciavardone, my ever-supportive spiritual siblings. Dr. Robin McFee, M.D., my trusted friend, fellow writer and personal Watson. Merideth "Diva" Kelley, Chelle Farrand, and the entire Baurdo Clan. Jenn, you kept me limber. Mary, you kept me sane. Tom, thanks for the wine. Lillie, you are the best apprentice a gal could ask for—I look forward to standing in line one day for a signed copy of your book(s)! To Penny Havard, my friend, teacher and costumer extraordinaire. Thank you for making me look so good in those accurate reproduction dresses! To Juanita Babcock, Fran Muller, Louisa Watrous, Julie Soto and Anne Collier. To Joanie DiMartino (Soup & Sonnets Forever!). To Swati and Kapil Jahn. And to

Marina Lindsay, Jaime and David Grounsell (under whose roof this novel was completed), Carolyne and Steve Sullivan, and all of my friends in England. From my heart, I thank you one and all for believing in me.

As a child, I was often told that no one would ever listen to me. I guess the old saying is true, only a fool believes everything they hear.

Jennifer M. Emerson

"At age seven, I read *A Christmas Carol*. I fell in love with London, its past, and with Dickens's stories. I am still in love."

Jennifer is a member of the London and Connecticut branches of the Dickens Fellowship, and the Friends of Dickens New York. On February 7th, 2012, she attended the wreath laying ceremony commemorating Dickens's 200th birthday at his grave in Westminster Abbey. The summer of 2013 marked her fourth research trip to London, during which time she was welcomed as a Volunteer Interpreter at The Charles Dickens House Museum, and attended the plaque unveiling of Dickens's first London home—in the shadow of the Cleveland Street Workhouse. This novel was completed during that trip.

A 19th Century Living History playwright and performer with over a decade of experience in Museum Interpretation, Jennifer also holds a Master of Fine Arts in Creative Writing from Fairfield University. She enjoys the challenge and excitement of bringing history and literature alive for a modern audience in fun, fresh and believable ways.

Bibliography & Further Reading

Ackroyd, Peter. *Dickens.* HarperCollins, 1990.

Dickens-Hawksley, Lucinda. *Charles Dickens – Dickens Bicentenary 1812-2012.* Insight Editions, 2011.

Dickens-Hawksley, Lucinda. *Katey.* London: Doubleday, 2006.

Hartley, Jenny. *Charles Dickens and the House of Fallen Women.* London: Methuen, 2008.

Johnson, Edgar. *The Heart of Charles Dickens.* New York: Duell, Sloan and Pearce, 1952.

Korg, Jacob. *London in Dickens's Day.* Englewood Cliffs, NJ: Prentice-Hall, 1960.

Mankowitz, Wolf. *Dickens of London.* New York: Macmillan (1st Edition), 1982.

Perdue, David. *Charles Dickens Webpage*: charlesdickenspage.com

Richardson, Ruth. *Dickens & the Workhouse (Oliver Twist & the London Poor).* Oxford University Press, 2012.

Slater, Michael. *Charles Dickens.* Yale University Press, 2009.

Dickens and the Whore

Made in the USA
Middletown, DE
03 February 2015